York

Saving

Nestled in a valley of the Yorkshire Dales is the quaint village of Burndale, home to a very special veterinary surgery and its dedicated staff who care for and heal local pets and surrounding farm animals. Run by dashing Dr. Archer Forde, things at this quiet little clinic have always been straightforward—definitely not rumor mill worthy. Until the arrival of two new additions sets tongues wagging—and hearts racing!

Archer and vet nurse Halley were only supposed to have one night together, no strings attached.
But now they have two surprises in store. Not only is Archer Halley's new boss, she's also carrying his baby!

After the loss of his wife, single dad James moves back to Yorkshire for his little daughter Tilly's sake. Joining his old friend Archer at Burndale Veterinary Surgery is just the fresh start he needs. A romantic entanglement is not! And yet the sparks that fly with vet Jenny are unexpected—and undeniable…

Escape to the country, rescue puppies and fall in love with the Yorkshire Village Vets!

Bound by Their Pregnancy Surprise by Louisa Heaton

Sparks Fly with the Single Dad by Kate Hardy

Both available now!

Dear Reader,

When you're in the sandwich generation, sometimes it's a struggle to fit everything in. Your parents need you; your children need you; you have a busy job; and there just isn't time for anything else.

That's the position my hero and heroine are both in—Jenny's a vet who's trying to balance her career in the local veterinary partnership with looking after her frail mother, while James is trying to balance working as a vet and being a single dad to his daughter.

Jenny doesn't want the emotional upheaval of dating again, and James, while knowing that his daughter needs a mother, can't face another relationship after being widowed.

But, now they've both moved back to the village where they grew up in the Yorkshire Dales, they discover that they're a good team at work. Can they be just as good a team outside and make a multigenerational home for all of them?

Read on to find out!

With love,

Kate Hardy

SPARKS FLY WITH THE SINGLE DAD

———

KATE HARDY

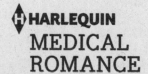

HARLEQUIN

MEDICAL
ROMANCE

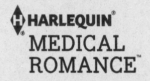

HARLEQUIN®
MEDICAL
ROMANCE™

Recycling programs
for this product may
not exist in your area.

ISBN-13: 978-1-335-59525-6

Sparks Fly with the Single Dad

Copyright © 2024 by Pamela Brooks

For questions and comments about the quality of this book,
please contact us at CustomerService@Harlequin.com.

Harlequin Enterprises ULC
22 Adelaide St. West, 41st Floor
Toronto, Ontario M5H 4E3, Canada
www.Harlequin.com

Printed in U.S.A.

Kate Hardy has always loved books and could read before she went to school. She discovered Harlequin books when she was twelve and decided that this was what she wanted to do. When she isn't writing, Kate enjoys reading, cinema, ballroom dancing and the gym. You can contact her via her website, katehardy.com.

Books by Kate Hardy

Harlequin Medical Romance

Twin Docs' Perfect Match

Second Chance with Her Guarded GP
Baby Miracle for the ER Doc

Surgeon's Second Chance in Florence
Saving Christmas for the ER Doc
An English Vet in Paris

Harlequin Romance

Snowbound with the Brooding Billionaire
One Week in Venice with the CEO
Crowning His Secret Princess
Tempted by Her Fake Fiancé
Wedding Deal with Her Rival

Visit the Author Profile page
at Harlequin.com for more titles.

For Louisa Heaton—it was such fun working with you and planning our duet!

Praise for
Kate Hardy

CHAPTER ONE

'So WHAT DID you want to talk to me about, Jenny?' Archer asked.

Jenny had deliberately waited until the rest of their colleagues had left Burndale Veterinary Surgery after their usual weekly meeting before tackling her business partner. He ought to hear this before anyone else did. 'I'm not sure whether I need to make you a mug of coffee or pour you a large whisky, first.'

'Neither. Just tell me,' Archer said.

'It's Mum,' Jenny said. Jenny had come back to Burndale from Leeds and joined the surgery here so she could keep a closer eye on her mum, knowing that Betty was terrified at the idea of going into a home and wanting to reassure her mum that she'd do her best to keep her in the house she'd lived in for decades. 'Robert came over, this weekend.'

'And?'

She blew out a breath. 'He thinks she's getting a lot worse. She needs more support. And he's got a point. Mum's not really safe to leave alone, any more—not so much the dementia, because that's still more at the forgetful stage than anything else and we can work round that, but she keeps falling, she won't use a walker and I'm worried she's going to end up with a serious fracture. I'm there at weekends and evenings, and I can get friends or our neighbour Sheila to sit with her if I'm called out for work. But I can't get more than three days a week for her in day-care, and I promised her I'd never put her in a nursing home. Which means I need to go part-time for a while.' Until…

No. She couldn't face that.

'I've spent this week exploring every avenue, and I'm coming up blank. Bottom line, it's me or me to pick up the slack.'

'Your brother can't help at all?' Archer asked, his tone deceptively mild.

She knew what he was thinking. Her best friend had said the same thing: Robert had dumped all their mum's care on her. But Jenny knew it wasn't a fight she could win, and she preferred to be practical. The most important thing was keeping her mum safe and as well as possible. 'It's a two-hour drive each way for him. Given the kind of pressure GPs are under, I don't think he'd be able to split the difference with me and do even one day a week.'

'He wouldn't consider doing what you did, and move closer to her?'

'There are the children to think about. It's not a great time for them to move schools.' And it was reasonable to consider the kids' needs before her mum's. After all, Jenny was the childless one. The divorced one. The one who'd have time to spare to look after their mother. She sighed. 'I'm sorry, Arch. I feel really horrible putting pressure on you. Not to mention the fact that it's not really that long since Max retired and I became your partner. But, unless someone invents a way for me to print a working 3-D model of myself, I need to drop down to three days a week at the practice.'

'When?'

She grimaced. 'This is the bad bit. As soon as possible. Within the next month, tops.'

'It's fine. Don't worry,' Archer said, and the lead weight that had been pushing down on Jenny's shoulders ever since her brother's visit finally started to lighten. 'I'll sort it out. We can get a locum in until we can find another vet—someone part-time, or even full-time to give us some extra flexibility.'

'Thanks, Archer. I really appreciate this.' She gave him a bearhug. If anyone had told her twenty years ago that the quiet, gangly lad with his shock of frizzy hair who was two years above her at school would turn out to be one of her closest friends as well as her business partner, she would've been surprised. Jenny had always known that Archer Forde was one of the good guys; but, since she'd come home to Burndale, she'd discovered just how nice he was.

Though they'd never be more than good friends. Yes, Archer was attractive: he'd filled out and got a decent haircut, and nowadays he was very easy on the eye. But there was no chemistry between them. He felt more like a big brother—and, though she felt disloyal thinking it, Jenny knew that her business partner was a lot more supportive than her own big brother was.

'I don't know how to thank you,' she said.

'It's what friends are for,' he said. 'You'd look out for me, if I was in your shoes.'

'Yes,' she agreed. 'Of course I would.'

'Then stop worrying. It's all fixable. Now, go home and make a fuss of your mum.'

'Thanks, Arch.' Jenny wished she could wave a magic wand for him, too. She knew how lonely he was; he'd admitted to her that since he'd lost Amy, his girlfriend, to a brain tumour, he just hadn't wanted to get involved with anyone else.

There were dozens of women who'd jump at the chance to date Burndale's most eligible bachelor, though Jenny wasn't going to insult her friend by trying to fix him up with someone. When he was ready to move on, then maybe she'd give him a nudge or two. But the best thing she could do right now was to have his back, the way he had hers. 'I'll see you tomorrow.'

Maybe now was the right time to move from London, James thought. Before Tilly started school, so she'd have a few months to settle in and make friends at nursery. His family would be thrilled if he went back to Burndale, and Tilly could grow up in the same beautiful countryside that he had. Yes, it would mean a longer trip for Anna's parents whenever they wanted to see their granddaughter, but he'd make sure to find a place big enough for them to stay whenever they wanted to visit.

The idea had been bubbling in the back of his head for a month now, ever since the incident with Sophie, their former nanny. But, before he set things officially in motion, it would be sensible to talk it over with someone else. Someone he'd known for years, and who'd been through the same kind of heartache he had. Someone who avoided relationships for exactly the same reason that he did, because he couldn't face a loss that deep ever again.

'Well, if it isn't Mr Herriot in London,' Archer greeted him when he joined the video-call.

'Indeed, Mr Herriot in Yorkshire,' James teased back. As schoolkids, they'd both fallen in love with the vet's stories, and with them both being science nerds it was obvious that they'd both end up training as veterinary surgeons and following in the footsteps of their hero. 'How's things?'

'Usual. You?'

'Hmm,' James said. 'I've been thinking. Maybe it'd be better for Tilly to grow up outside London.'

'You're moving?' Archer looked surprised.

'I'm seriously thinking about it.'

'What's brought that on?'

James groaned, and told Archer about the incident with the nanny.

Archer winced. 'Ouch.'

'Even if she hadn't walked out on us, the next morning, it was obviously she couldn't stay. Not after that. I've got a temp nanny covering for her, but all this change isn't great for Tilly. She needs stability. And it's made me think. Maybe now's the right time to move.' He took a deep breath. 'This isn't me asking you to give me a job, Arch, because I know you've got Jenny in the partnership and you don't really need a third vet in Burndale. But often people talk about advertising a post before they actually do it, so I wondered if you'd heard of any vet's jobs going within, I dunno, half an hour's drive of Burndale?'

'You're coming back to live in Burndale?' Archer's eyes widened, and then he smiled. 'You know what, James—I think we could do each other a favour.'

'What do you need?' James asked immediately. 'The answer's yes.'

'You're going to get me a visit to the International Space Station for my birthday?' Archer teased.

'If I could, you know it'd be yours,' James said, laughing back.

'Strictly between you and me, because we haven't announced it yet, Jenny's going part time,' Archer said.

'Because of her mum?' James asked, having heard about Jenny's situation from his own mother.

'Yes. I told her I'd get a locum in while I look for someone to fill in the gap permanently. But, if you're serious about coming back to Burndale, you could save me all the recruitment hassle.' Archer looked hopefully at him. 'I can offer you anything between two days a week and a full-time post—we'll work round everyone's needs.'

'That,' James said, 'would be brilliant. Yes. Yes, *please.*'

'That's great. When can you start?' Archer asked.

'I'll talk to the senior partner here tomorrow,' James said. 'They know my situation, so they might agree to use a locum and release me early. I'll call you as soon as I've talked to them. Then we can work out which days you need me and what childcare I need to put in place for Tilly around nursery hours—I don't expect Mum or my sister Vicky to pick up all the slack.'

'Perfect.' Archer smiled. 'It'll be so good to actually work with you, after all these years. Jenny's a sweetheart, so you'll fit in to the practice really well. Plus you'll know nearly all the clients.'

'I'm looking forward to working with you, too. If Anna's job hadn't been in London, I probably would've suggested us going into partnership years ago,' James said.

'I nearly asked you to join us when Max retired,' Archer admitted, 'but I thought you wanted to stay in London.'

Where James could take flowers to Anna every Friday, just as he had when she'd been alive: except nowadays it was to her grave rather than waltzing into the kitchen, handing over the flowers and getting a kiss in return. 'I did,' James said, pushing the sadness down. 'But I have to put Tilly's needs first. And I think it's time for us to come home.'

Archer's smile was slightly tight; James knew his best friend was thinking about the strained relationship he'd had with his own mother, plus his absent father. Archer's mother had never put her kids first, and Archer's brother Axle had really struggled. 'Yes.

You *do* have to put her needs first,' Archer said. 'Call me tomorrow and let me know what your boss says.' His smile broadened. 'And I can't wait to welcome you to Burndale Veterinary Surgery.'

Three weeks later, James dropped Tilly at the nursery in Burndale for her second session.

'Daddy, don't go!' she said, clutching his hand tightly as they stood outside the door. 'I don't want to stay here. I want to go with you.'

He knelt down next to her and wrapped his arms round her. 'Hey, you had a nice time here yesterday. You made new friends and you painted that lovely picture. You'll have a nice time today, too,' he said. 'And Granny will be here to pick you up this afternoon.'

A tear trickled down her cheek. 'But I miss Jas.'

Jasminder was Tilly's best friend at the nursery she'd gone to in London. 'We'll call her tonight, before tea,' he promised. 'She's still your best friend and that's not going to change, just because we moved here. Look at me and Uncle Archer—we've been best friends ever since we were at school together. It didn't make any difference to us being best friends when he came back here while I went to London.'

Another tear trickled down Tilly's cheek, and James's heart squeezed. But he couldn't tear himself in two. Just how did women manage to do this? he wondered. Would Anna have been better at teaching Tilly how to be independent? Was he letting his late wife down as well as his daughter?

'Tilly, I love you very much and of course I want to be with you,' he said gently. 'But I have some poorly animals who are waiting for me to make them better. Can you be brave and let me do that?'

She looked at him with her huge brown eyes under a mop of dark ringlets, so reminiscent of her mother's. 'Yes, Daddy.'

'That's my girl,' he said, and gave her a hug. 'Let's go in.'

Once Tilly was happily sitting at a table, making a dog out of bright pink playdough, James headed for the surgery.

Barb, the receptionist, looked up with a smile as he walked in.

'If it isn't young James Madden. Welcome home, love,' she said.

'Thank you, Barb. It's good to be back,' he said.

Archer appeared from his consulting room. 'Welcome to the practice,' he said. 'You obviously remember Barb, our receptionist. Come and meet the others.'

James followed Archer through to the back rooms.

'James, this is Anu, our vet nurse,' Archer said. 'And you remember Jenny Sutton— Braithwaite, as she was when we were at school.'

'Nice to meet you, Anu,' James said, shaking her hand. 'Jenny. Good to see you again.' He smiled at her and shook her hand; to his surprise, it felt as if an electric shock shimmered across his skin where it touched hers.

What the...?

He'd never had that much to do with Jenny at school. She'd been two years younger than him and in a completely different friendship group; and he'd dated only sporadically in sixth form because he'd been focused on getting the grades to read veterinary medicine at university. Like him, she'd moved away after university. He did remember Jenny, but only vaguely. He certainly hadn't expected to be so aware of the bluest eyes he'd ever seen.

'Nice to see you again, too,' she said politely. 'I'm sorry to hear about what happened to your wife.'

The village grapevine had probably filled her in—or at least given her more than the barest-bones information that Archer might have told her. How Anna had died from an amniotic embolism after the caesarean section when Tilly was born; it was an incredibly rare event, and it had knocked James for six, losing his wife and coping with being a single dad to their new-born daughter all at the same time.

'Thank you,' he said.

'Is your daughter settling in OK?' Jenny asked.

'We had a few tears this morning when I dropped her off at nursery,' he said. 'Tilly misses her friends from ho — from London,' he corrected himself. Burndale was home, now. 'She'll get there.'

'And she starts school in September?' At his nod, Jenny said, 'My best friend, Tamsin, is the deputy head of the infant school. I can have a word with her, if you like, to see if she can give you a heads-up on who's likely to be in her class, so you can sort out some playdates over the summer to help Tilly make friends and settle in.'

'That'd be great. Thank you.' He paused. 'How's your mum doing?'

Jenny gave him a rueful smile. 'Village grapevine filled you in, too?'

'Of course,' he said. Plus, as one of the practice vets, he'd needed to know that she wasn't available on Thursdays and Fridays. Archer had given him the barest bones: enough so that James understood Jenny's situation, but no gossipy details.

'Mum's torn between being relieved that I'm going to be home with her another two days a week, and guilty that she's sabotaging my career. Which she absolutely isn't. It was my choice to go part-time,' Jenny said.

'If it helps, I would've done the same, in your shoes,' he said.

'It's hard to juggle, sometimes,' she said. 'Though I guess it's just as hard juggling things as a single dad.'

'Worrying about whether you're doing the best for them. Tell me about it,' he said with a smile.

'Well, I guess we have patients waiting,' she said. 'Catch you later.'

James's first patient was a springer spaniel with a nicked leg. Mrs Martin, his owner, had fashioned a temporary dressing of lint and micropore tape over the cut. 'I feel terrible,' she said. 'We were giving Alfie a haircut last night—he hates going to the groomers, so we've got our own low-noise clippers and we can keep reassuring him and giving him a break when he needs it. But you know how long hair can get matted—there was a bit on his back leg where we thought we'd better use scissors.' She winced. 'He wriggled, and my husband accidentally nicked him. Alfie didn't make a sound—we didn't even realise what had happened until we saw blood running down his leg.'

'At least his leg wasn't caught on rusty wire, so we don't have to worry so much about infection,' James said. 'When did it happen?'

'Last night. We put a dressing on it, but I wanted to get him checked over properly.'

'That's always a good idea if you're worried—or if the cut's bigger than a couple of centimetres.' James made a fuss of the dog, then removed the dressing and examined the wound. 'It's going to need stitching, I'm afraid,' he said. 'Though it might be a tricky repair. Skin heals best if we stitch it within a couple of hours of the wound happening.'

Mrs Martin looked stricken, and made a fuss of her dog. 'Oh, my poor boy. I wish

I'd called you last night. Is he going to be all right?'

'The cut's in a difficult place,' James said. 'Not so much for me stitching it, but because of the way the muscles move here—it's harder for the stitches to hold the skin in place, plus the flap of skin here is pointing upwards instead of down.' When she bit her lip, he added, 'I can do it—but Alfie will definitely need a collar to stop him licking the stitches and taking them out, because the repair will be quite fragile and we need to give it a chance to heal. When did he last eat?'

'Last night. He had some water about six o'clock this morning—I didn't take him for his usual walk before breakfast,' Mrs Martin said. 'And I held off on breakfast in case he needed stitches.'

'That was the best thing you could've done,' James said, making another fuss of the dog. 'Well, gorgeous boy. We'll be keeping you in, this morning, and I'll sort your leg out at the end of morning surgery. We'll give you a call, Mrs Martin, and let you know when he's round and again when you can collect him.'

A tear leaked down her face. 'He's going to be all right?'

'We'll do our best. But remember you can

always come in and see the vet nurse here if there's a bit of matted hair and we can sort it out for you,' he said, as gently as he could. 'That'll save any future issues like this.'

'My husband's never going to be allowed near a pair of scissors, ever, *ever* again,' she said, and made another fuss of her dog. 'I'll see you soon, Alf. Be a good—' Her voice broke. 'I'm sorry. My daughter left home six weeks ago and I haven't got used to the empty nest, yet. Alfie's kind of taken over as…' She shook her head. 'I know it sounds daft, but he's like my youngest child.'

'That's how a lot of people feel about their pets,' James reassured her. 'We'll take good care of him, Mrs Martin.' James took the dog's lead, but Alfie whimpered and tried to follow his owner out of the room.

'This way, boy,' James said gently but firmly, and led the spaniel into the area at the back where they kennelled animals waiting for an operation.

Jenny grabbed a coffee mid-morning in her break between appointments, adding cold water to it so she could drink it straight down.

She was still shocked by her response that morning to James.

Although they hadn't been in the same friendship group at school, she'd noticed the good-looking teenager back then. She'd really liked his green eyes and his smile, and the way his dark hair flopped over his forehead—just like Orlando Bloom's, her favourite actor at the time—but she'd been way too shy to dare ask him out. He was two years above her. If he'd said no, she would never have lived it down among her own year, and the idea of the relentless teasing had been too daunting. And he'd never seemed to notice her, though maybe it was because he always had his head in his books.

With James being Archer's best friend she'd got to know him by proxy since she'd been working with Archer. Like her, James was single and focused on his family's needs—though in his case it was through being widowed rather than divorced.

And she really couldn't face dating again anyway. The break-up of her seven-year marriage had left her bruised. It had been amicable, to a point—she and Simon hadn't ended up sniping at each other, and they'd been fair in dividing their assets—but, now she looked back, she realised she'd always gone along with what he wanted instead of pushing for more of a middle way.

They'd met as students, but even then Simon had always been much more ambitious than she was, adamant that he didn't want children because he wanted to focus on his career. He'd made consultant at a young age and made a real name for himself in Leeds; Jenny had come to terms with the fact that as they'd got older she'd wanted a family but he hadn't. She had her niece and nephew, even though she didn't see as much of them as she'd like.

The job in London, two years ago, had been the tipping point. He hadn't even told her he'd applied for it—just assumed that she'd go along with him. But, when her mother had been diagnosed with early-stage Alzheimer's, how could Jenny have possibly deserted her?

She didn't regret choosing her family over her marriage, but she sometimes wished that Simon had been prepared to help her find a compromise that worked for all of them. That he'd been there for her to lean on, share her worries and reassure her. But it wasn't who he was, and she knew it was pointless wishing otherwise.

And now she'd met James again. Felt a spark of attraction she hadn't expected to feel again, for someone who had just as many complications in his personal life. Neither of them had time to date someone between work and caring for their closest family member. She'd just have to ignore the attraction and focus on having a good working relationship with him. Keep it professional, she reminded herself. Don't think about how his dark hair flops over his forehead. Or how beautiful his mouth is when he smiles. Or how his eyes are the same green of the moors on a spring day.

All the same, when James caught up with her after morning surgery, awareness of him quivered up her spine.

'I need to repair a tricky cut on a spaniel,' James said. 'Fancy being my anaesthetist?'

Working together would be the best way to help her damp down that attraction and keep it professional, she thought. 'Sure.'

Except she quickly discovered that she'd been very, very wrong.

Seeing the kindness with which James treated the spaniel, his green eyes crinkling at the corners as he made a fuss of the dog before shaving Alfie's paw ready for the anaesthetic injection, made her heart melt.

Seeing the deftness of his hands when the dog was on the operating table and James stitched up the cut—which was indeed in a tricky place—made her wonder how those hands might feel against her skin.

And seeing the smile on his face when she reversed the anaesthesia and the dog woke up made her stomach flutter.

'Good job,' she said, to cover her confusion.

'Good teamwork,' he corrected. 'Though if that had had been any deeper, it would've involved his Achilles' tendon.'

Which, she knew, would've been life-limiting. The spaniel would've been miserable, unable to race around and bounce about as the breed usually did. 'He was lucky,' she said.

'Thanks for your help,' he said, and gently scratched the top of the spaniel's head. 'And I need to phone your mum, Alfie,' he added to the spaniel, 'so she can stop worrying.'

Oh, that smile. It'd charm the hardest heart in the village. And it was definitely doing things to her.

'I'll catch you later,' she said. 'And I'll have a word with Tamsin tonight about school.'

'I appreciate that,' he said. 'Thank you, Jenny.' His eyes crinkled at the corners, again making her feel that weird little fluttering in her stomach. Just like she'd had when she'd known him as a teenager.

She was going to have to be really, really careful not to let herself fall for James.

CHAPTER TWO

'OF COURSE I can suggest people James could get in touch with to sort out a play date,' Tamsin said. 'Give him my number, and I can give him all the info about applying for school places, too.'

'Thanks, Tam.' Jenny smiled.

'How are you getting on with him at the practice?'

'Fine,' Jenny said. 'He's a nice guy.'

Although she'd willed herself not to blush, clearly it hadn't worked because Tamsin gave her an arch look. 'Like that, is it?'

'No. We're colleagues. Friends,' Jenny said. Even though she knew it sounded as if she was protesting a bit too much. 'He's a single dad and doesn't need the hassle of a relationship.'

'Just like you're a carer to your mum and don't need the hassle of a relationship.'

'Exactly,' Jenny said.

Tamsin poured more wine into their glasses. 'You know, it sounds to me as if you both need a bit of fun.'

Not sure where this was going, Jenny didn't answer.

'Jen, it's been two years since you and Simon split up. It's time you made a bit of time for *you* in your life. If he likes you and you like him, why not go out together?'

'Because I don't need the complication of a relationship—I can't leave Mum in the evenings,' she said, knowing it was probably an excuse, but not wanting to admit to how daunting it felt to date again. How did you even meet anyone when you were in your thirties, unless you used a dating app? And anyone she met would have as much emotional baggage as she did. She'd heard so many horror stories. She really couldn't face it. 'Plus he's still grieving for Anna.'

'Or maybe,' Tamsin said, 'it's easier for him to let people think that, and then nobody's going to nag him to get out there and find someone to share his life.'

'Like you nag me,' Jenny grumbled, though she knew her best friend meant well—and probably had a point. 'And he has Tilly to think about.'

'He's just moved back to the village from London—it's common knowledge that he's staying with his parents until his lease starts on the cottage in Richmond Road, and his mum will jump at the chance to spend some time with her granddaughter. And I,' Tamsin said, 'am very happy to come and have a cup of tea and a natter with your mum while you go out for a drink or whatever with James.'

'I...' Jenny knew she should have all kinds of excuses ready to go. But they'd all fallen out of her head.

'You like him,' Tamsin said, 'and he likes you.'

'How could you possibly know that?' Jenny protested. 'Of course he doesn't.'

'Jenny, you're gorgeous. Of course he likes you. Look at you. You're fit from all the physical stuff you do with animals, you're beautiful, there's all that silky blonde hair men would just love to twirl round their fingers, and nobody's going to resist those lovely blue eyes of yours. Don't argue,' Tamsin said firmly. 'Simon needed his head examining, putting his career before you.'

'It wasn't his fault.'

Tamsin scoffed. 'It certainly wasn't yours. He could've had a perfectly good career in Leeds. Commuting between here and Leeds wouldn't have killed him.'

'He would've been crazy to turn down that opportunity in London. It was everything he wanted.'

'He didn't even *try* to compromise, Jenny,' Tamsin said, looking cross. 'He didn't consider there were two of you in that marriage with a good career. Or think that you had opportunities, like the partnership you were offered but turned down because he wanted to live in Leeds. And why didn't he suggest your mum moved in with you in Leeds? He was completely selfish.'

Jenny was uncomfortably aware that it was true. Then again, she hadn't stood up to him, had she? 'It's worked out for the best,' she said. 'I'm a partner in the practice here, and Mum hasn't had to move from the place that's been her home for forty-five years.'

Tamsin sighed. 'OK. I know I'm not going to win *that* battle. But I'm going to win this one, Jenny. All right, I accept you're not in a place right now where you have time for a proper relationship, and neither is James. But some no-strings fun…that'd do you both a lot of good. You've both had a tough time and you deserve a break.'

'I'm fine as I am,' Jenny said.

'No, you're not,' Tamsin said. 'You're doing your best for your mum, you work hard—and you don't have any time left for you.'

'I'm *fine*,' Jenny repeated stubbornly.

And she was. Until the next morning, when James performed the sedation so she could do a diagnostic X-ray on a ginger and white cat.

'What's your thinking?' James asked.

'Sally's—his owner's—mother-in-law came to stay for a couple of days and left her knitting out,' Jenny said.

'Ah. And Pekoe here couldn't resist batting the ball of wool about.'

'Last night,' Jenny confirmed. 'Then, this morning, he wasn't very well. He was vomiting, refusing food and just couldn't seem to get comfortable. Sally's mother-in-law took over Sally's shift in the tea shop so Sally could bring him in for us to have a look at. And when she told me about the playing with wool stuff last night, it made me wonder if we're looking at a linear foreign body.' She blew out a breath. 'I couldn't see any wool caught at the back of his mouth—hence the X-ray, to see what's going on in his stomach.'

The X-ray showed the classic 'string of pearls' sign, indicating that one end of a piece of wool had become trapped in the stomach while the other end had moved through the cat's gastrointestinal tract, and the cat's intestines had bunched up on themselves around the wool, a bit like a concertina.

'Classic presentation of an LFB,' James observed. 'Poor chap. No wonder he wasn't feeling well.'

'Let's just hope the wool hasn't cut through his intestinal wall,' Jenny said. A perforated intestine could be life-threatening. Thankfully Pekoe was only nine years old so he had a better chance than an elderly, less robust cat. Jenny palpated his stomach and intestines. 'I can't feel where the wool's caught.'

'So we're not looking at a simple dislodgement of the wool where we can remove it through Pekoe's mouth,' James said.

'I need to open him up. Ready to go with full anaesthesia?' Jenny asked.

'Yes.' Deftly, he intubated the cat and increased the anaesthesia.

Once the cat was fully anaesthetised, Jenny opened his abdomen at the point where the X-ray suggested it was the most likely place where the wool was stuck.

'Can you see it?' James asked.

'I've found it—and there's no sign of perforation,' Jenny said with relief. She gently dislodged the wool, and managed to remove it. 'And that's good. Just the one cut in his intestines, so he'll heal more quickly,' she said, stitching the cat's intestines with dissolvable stitches before suturing his skin closed. 'Pekoe's definitely used up one of his nine lives this week.'

'Pekoe.' James looked at the cat and smiled. 'Was he named for Orange Pekoe tea, do you think?'

Jenny laughed. 'Given that Sally owns the village tea shop, what do you think?'

James laughed back. 'That's the perfect name for him.'

'We'll keep him in for observations for the next forty-eight hours,' she said, once James had brought the cat round, 'and I'll ring Sally to let her know that he's going to be OK.'

'That'll be the best phone call she has all year,' James said with a smile. 'And that's the lovely bit of our job, telling owners everything's going to be fine.'

'I hate breaking bad news,' Jenny said. 'You can tell what kind of cases I've had in a week, just from my chocolate consumption.'

'I know what you mean,' James said. 'It's so hard for owners saying goodbye—but the good ones remember the love their pet gave them over all the years. They sit with their pet to the end and let them go to sleep in their arms.'

Jenny had to blink away the tears at the thought, and turned away to make a fuss of the still-woozy cat.

'You've got a soft spot for cats, then?' James asked.

'I know you're not supposed to have favourite animals,' Jenny said, 'but I always think of Mum whenever we have cats in. She'd be lost without Sooty.' Or, rather, even more lost than she was gradually becoming, and the knot of worry tightened in her stomach. She shook herself. 'Ignore me.'

As if James could read her thoughts, he said, 'It's tough, seeing your parents become more frail.'

'Especially because Dad died five years ago,' Jenny said. 'It was his heart. Mum started to go downhill about then. My brother Robert and I thought it was grief and a bit of support would help. Except then we realised things were getting more serious.'

'Grief can make you shut everyone and everything out,' James said.

Jenny winced. Of course James was talking from first-hand experience about being widowed. 'Sorry, James. I didn't mean to stamp on a sore spot.'

'You didn't,' he said. 'It's something I've noticed with our older patients—when they're on their own, their pets are that little bit more precious. But, since you raised the topic of grief and loneliness, Anna and I loved each other and we were happy. I'm sad she's gone, and I'm sadder still that Tilly will only get to see and hear her mum in photos and videos. Living in London, we didn't have pets, so I think I would've shut the world out if I hadn't had Tilly depending on me.' He wrinkled his nose. 'What I'm trying to say, in a very clumsy way, is that you have a point about grief making people disconnected from others.'

'It must be hard, coming to terms with what happened to Anna.' It was her turn to wrinkle her nose. 'Sorry. I didn't mean to pry.'

'You're not prying. Most people avoid the subject,' he said. 'What can you say to someone whose partner died in their thirties? And you're right. It's hard to come to terms with it. I'm not a doctor, but I'm a vet and I read every pregnancy book going when Anna was expecting Tilly. Why didn't I notice something sooner?'

'As you said, you're not a doctor,' Jenny said gently. 'It's such a rare complication, half the staff on the ward had maybe seen one case before, if that. You've got nothing to feel guilty about.'

'Mmm,' James said. 'And Tilly has to come first. I'm not going to spend my time wallowing in grief when she needs me. And I'm wallowing now.' He rolled his eyes. 'Tell you what. To make up for my utter rubbishness just now, let me buy you a coffee and a sandwich for lunch, and you can tell Sally the good news in person rather than ringing her.'

'You d—' Jenny began, and stopped herself.

Tamsin had a point.

She worked hard, she looked after her mum, and she needed to make a little bit of time for herself. Becoming friends with James—or maybe even some no-strings dating—would be good for both of them. 'Thank you,' she said. 'That'd be nice. Maybe we can get Archer to join us.'

'Great idea,' James said with another of those stomach-flipping smiles.

Except Archer had been called away to see

a sick cow, so it turned out to be just the two of them for a quick sandwich and coffee in Sally's tea shop.

'Pekoe's really going to be OK?' Sally stifled a sob and hugged Jenny. 'Thank you. Thank you so much. He's nine, and I've had him since he was a kitten. I can't imagine life without him.'

'I'm keeping him in for a couple of days,' Jenny warned. 'He needs pain relief, IV fluids and medications to control nausea and help his intestines get moving again.'

'And then, when he does come home, you need to keep him quiet,' James added. 'It'll take another week and a half for the incisions to heal—and he'll need to come back to have the external stitches out.'

'The internal ones don't need removing,' Jenny said. 'They'll take about four months to dissolve fully, and in the meantime they'll support his intestines.'

'My poor little lad,' Sally said. 'Ian's mum would never have forgiven herself if…' Her voice thickened with tears again.

'He's not the first cat to have swallowed a bit of wool, and he won't be the last,' Jenny said.

'But, yes, you need to keep a close eye

on wool, ribbons, tinsel and the like,' James added. 'They're a magnet for cats—and they can cause a lot of damage.'

'We'll definitely keep a closer eye, in future,' Sally said. She smiled at them. 'You two are obviously close; you virtually finish each other's sentences.'

Jenny could feel heat rising in her face. 'We've both done the job for a long time and we've seen a lot of similar cases,' she said. 'We just think along the same professional lines.'

'Exactly,' James said. 'We're friends. Or becoming that way,' he added. 'We kind of know each other already through Archer.'

'Absolutely,' she agreed firmly.

Once Sally had sorted out their sandwiches and coffee, they found a table in the sunny courtyard.

'Sorry about—well, what Sally said,' Jenny said, embarrassment flooding through her but knowing she needed to make things clear between them to avoid any future awkwardness.

'That's the only thing about living in a small village,' James said. 'They mean well, but everyone sees a single person and they start matchmaking, even though you don't want them to.'

'Tell me about it,' Jenny said feelingly. 'I don't have any designs on you, just as I realise you don't have any designs on me.'

'Exactly,' James said. 'And not making boundaries clear is part of the reason I ended up leaving London.'

It was none of her business, but she said awkwardly, 'Anything you tell me won't go any further.'

'Thank you,' he said, and raked a hand through his hair. 'Actually, it'd be good to get a female point of view, if you don't mind me using you as a sounding board. I couldn't face telling Mum or my sister, because I feel such a fool.'

'I think we've all been there at some point. OK. I'm listening,' she said.

'We had a live-in nanny in London, to cover the gaps between my work hours and Tilly's nursery hours. I was grateful for her help, and I made the mistake of telling her.'

Jenny frowned. 'Why was that a mistake? Everyone likes to be appreciated.'

'Because she took it the wrong way,' James said dryly. 'She thought I meant more than just her job. One evening, I went out for a meal with the others in my practice because Sophie—the nanny—had agreed to babysit for me. But, when I got home, she was waiting for me…in my bed, without a stitch on.'

Jenny winced. 'Awkward.'

'Really, *really* awkward,' James said. 'I didn't know where to look. So I shut my eyes, apologised to her, and explained that I wasn't looking for a relationship—between work and Tilly, I simply don't have space for anything else.'

Exactly as Jenny had told Tamsin: and now she'd had it confirmed. Part of her was relieved, because it would mean he understood her own position; but a little part of her was wistful. How ridiculous had she been, wondering what it would be like to date James, just as she had fantasised about when she'd been a teenager? Better to stick to what he'd said to Sally: they were on their way to becoming friends, and that was it. 'What happened then?' she asked.

'She…um…wasn't very happy about it. I asked her very politely to get dressed and leave my room, and said we'd discuss the way forward in the morning when we'd both had time to think and cool down. And I was sorry if I'd led her to think I regarded her as anything other than as Tilly's nanny.' He winced. 'Obviously I went downstairs and gave her a lot of time to…um…get dressed and out of my bed. The next morning, I found a note from her propped against the kettle with her door key beside it. She said in the circumstances she thought I'd understand that she wanted to leave immediately, and she wasn't prepared to work a notice period.'

'You're kidding. She didn't say goodbye to Tilly before she left?' Jenny asked, shocked that the nanny would abandon her charge like that.

'No.' His mouth tightened. 'Obviously Tilly was upset when I had to tell her that Sophie wasn't going to be around any more. She asked if Sophie had gone to heaven, like Mummy had.' He shook his head. 'God, I know it would've been embarrassing for her, having to face me after she'd made such a blatant move and I'd turned her down. It wouldn't have been great for me, either. But surely Sophie could've put Tilly first and realised how it might affect her?' He blew out a breath. 'Anyway, I told Tilly that Sophie hadn't gone to heaven. It was just that another family needed her to look after them, and she hadn't had time to say goodbye, and we'd find someone else who could look after her when I was at work.'

'It sounds to me as if you handled it the best way possible. Was Tilly OK?' Jenny asked.

'Tearful for a few days, but thankfully she was OK. Luckily my boss was very understanding and told me to take a couple of days off until I could find a temporary nanny, and our admin manager's sister worked at an agency and found a couple of people Tilly liked who could fit us in. But the upheaval made me think about how I'd manage when Tilly started school. The more I thought about it, the more it made me want to come back to Burndale, so I'd got the support of my family as a safety net.'

'When does she start school? September?' Jenny asked.

'January,' he said, 'because she isn't four until the middle of August and she'll be one of the younger ones in the year. I thought about it, and it makes sense to move now and let her get settled in. I rang Archer to see if he knew of any jobs going up this way, and that's when he told me about you needing to go part-time and suggested I join the practice.'

'On a purely selfish note, I'm so glad you did. It made me feel a lot less guilty about letting him down,' Jenny said. 'It's not that long since Max retired, and it wasn't fair of me to ask to go part-time so soon after becoming Archer's partner in the practice. I should've realised how bad the situation with Mum was getting, a lot earlier than I did.'

'When you're with someone every day, you don't notice the small, gradual changes,' James said. 'Don't beat yourself up about it.'

'That's much, much easier said than done,' Jenny said. 'But then I guess you've probably beaten yourself up about your situation with the nanny.'

'I have,' James admitted. 'I've gone over and over how I might have given Sophie the wrong impression, and I just can't see it.'

'What did you say to her, exactly?' Jenny asked.

He looked blank for a moment. 'I can't remember the exact words. I think I said something like I was grateful for her help and glad she was with us.'

'Hmm,' Jenny said. 'I think maybe if you'd said you were glad she got on so well with Tilly because you didn't have to worry about your little girl, it might've made it a bit clearer that you were talking about her in a professional capacity rather than a personal one.'

'There's such a fine line,' he said. 'I was never interested in her in *that* way. And if I had wanted to date her, I would've talked to her about it first and suggested she got another job, so it wasn't like me being a creepy employer expecting the nanny to…well. You know what I mean. Putting someone in an awkward position where they don't feel they can say no in case it affects their job. That's really not OK.' He blew out a breath. 'That's why I'm a bit wary of hiring another permanent nanny, in case I mess it up again—not give her the wrong idea, I mean, but I don't want to go too far the *other* way and make someone feel unwelcome.' He took a sip of coffee. 'I'm hoping that, between me and the nursery, we can cover Tilly's childcare without me needing to rely too much on Mum's help. I know she loves being with Tilly, but I don't want to take advantage of her. It isn't fair.'

'I'm pretty sure your mum understands your situation and she's only too pleased to help,' Jenny said. 'I know my mum would've been, in her shoes.'

'You don't have children?'

'Simon—my ex—didn't want children. He was very focused on his career,' Jenny said.

'And you were OK with that?'

'Yes,' she said, though it wasn't strictly true. 'I went through a broody stage in the first couple of years we were together,' she admitted, 'but he made it clear that he didn't want kids and that wasn't going to change. And I loved him and wanted to be with him, so I made the choice not to have kids.' She shrugged. 'And I love my job. It was fine, until he got the job offer in London. It was a really good opportunity— senior consultant in a London hospital with some teaching that could lead to a possible professorship. Of course he couldn't turn it down. But that's when I discovered my line in the sand: I didn't want to be so far away from Mum. Coming here from Leeds was enough of a trek to see her; coming here from London would've been even further.'

'Couldn't she have gone to London with you?'

If Simon hadn't wanted her mother to live with them in Leeds, he definitely wouldn't have wanted her around in London. 'No,' she said carefully. 'So I told him I was happy for him to go to London, but I couldn't go with him.'

'And he went without you?' James looked surprised.

'Yes.' It had been a shock—she'd hoped that the ultimatum might make him think of a different way forward. But it hadn't; he'd left her behind without a second glance. Though she knew that if he'd stayed, he would've grown to resent her and her mother. The split, painful as it had been, had definitely been the right decision. 'He's found a like-minded high-flyer, now, and they're happy.'

'And are you?'

'I'm fine,' she said, giving him the full-wattage smile she knew everyone expected to see from her but didn't quite feel.

James wasn't entirely convinced that Jenny was telling him the truth. There were shadows in her eyes that told him she shared the same bone-deep loneliness that he felt, the same worry that she was responsible for someone else's health and happiness and was so close to getting it wrong all the time.

And then there was the other thing.

The spark of awareness he felt, every time he saw her.

It was ridiculous. He didn't really know her; yet, at the same time, he'd known her for years. At school, where she'd been one of the girls two years below him; and then, when she'd come back to Burndale, he'd got to know her through what Archer had told him about her. She was a reliable, steady business partner who was easy to work with, good with the patients and their owners, and even charmed their older, more set in their ways clients who didn't think a woman was much use in a calving pen…until she'd proved them wrong by sorting out the difficult delivery they'd asked for help with, and topped it by drinking a mug of strong farmer's tea without wincing.

But it was more than that.

Jenny Sutton was the first woman he'd really noticed since Anna. Which made her dangerous to his peace of mind. Especially as he'd been so clueless about Sophie and the way she'd interpreted his words. What was to say he wouldn't get it wrong here, too?

Jenny had said she didn't have time for a relationship, and it was obvious that, between her job and caring for her mum, she had no time for herself. Just like him. So that made her safe…didn't it?

'It's hard to get the balance right, isn't it?' he asked. 'You put your little one in day-care, and you wonder if you're failing them and you should really be at home with them all the time.'

'It's the same with organising day-care for your parent—you worry you're doing the wrong thing, though you know it's good for them to have the chance to see others their own age, who've got similar life experiences and understand their situation,' she said. 'You feel that they looked after you when you needed them, so now it's your turn to do the same. But that'd mean giving up the career you've worked so hard to achieve, and if you do that you feel you're letting yourself down.'

'Whatever you do, it's wrong. No wonder they call us the sandwich generation,' James said. 'Small children and elderly parents— they have a lot in common.'

She nodded. 'You just do your best to fit in between family and your job. As for all the well-meaning people who suggest you join a dating app and find a partner, too—there just isn't time for it.'

'And then you feel guilty because maybe you're not doing enough. Maybe I should find a mum for Tilly, a partner for me to share my worries and love both of us,' he said.

'A partner who understands I want to look after my mum, share my worries and love both of us,' Jenny echoed.

'I'm assuming your ex…didn't?' He could've kicked himself for saying it, because she'd already pretty much told him that. 'Sorry. My social skills…um…need a bit of work.'

'No need to apologise. You're fine. Simon was a neurosurgeon,' she said. 'The exact man you'd want working on someone you loved, because he was utterly focused and brilliant at his job.'

'But not so brilliant when it came to family matters?' James guessed.

'It feels a bit disloyal to say so, and I don't mean it in a horrible or judgemental way, but Simon just wasn't a family man. When we first met, I was bowled over by his energy, and I didn't even think about anything else. Then, when I hit the broody stage, I discovered he wasn't—I'd thought we could combine a career and a family, but that wasn't what he wanted. And I loved him, so I went along with what he wanted,' Jenny said. 'And I'm guessing nobody can ever replace Anna for you.'

He blew out a breath. 'No. It's been nearly four years, now. Tilly's birthday is always bittersweet for me; I want to celebrate the joy of her arrival in my life.'

'But it's also the day you lost Anna.'

'It felt as if the sun went in and never came out from behind the clouds again,' he said. 'I miss her, even now. And I guess I've kind of used Tilly as a way not to deal with it—if I'm focused on being a dad, I don't have to think about my own loss.'

'You need to make time for you, too,' she said gently. 'And I'm fully aware of how much of a hypocrite I am.'

'Not a hypocrite, at all,' he said. 'Actually, you've made me feel better about it, because you do actually get where I'm coming from. It's the same for you, isn't it?'

'Not quite. It's only two years since we walked away from each other—and Simon's still around,' she corrected.

'And you miss him?'

'I miss the idea of him more than Simon himself. I miss what I wish he'd been for me,' Jenny said. 'Which is very messed up, I know.'

'And you haven't wanted to look at anyone else?'

'I don't want to take any risks. I got it wrong, last time; and I don't want Mum to be collateral damage if I get it wrong again. I'm guessing that's similar for you?'

He nodded. 'I don't want Tilly to be collateral damage. We're pretty much on the same page, I think.'

'You're right,' she said.

'The thing that scares me,' he said, 'is the

day Tilly works it out for herself—that her mum died on the day she was born. I've been practising my speech for that moment for years, to make sure she knows that Anna's death wasn't her fault. I know what I said to you earlier about why didn't I notice, but it really wasn't anyone's fault. Nobody could've predicted an amniotic embolism. And her mum would've loved her just as much as I do.' He swallowed hard. 'Just as much as I loved Anna herself. Even if I do find another partner, in years to come, I'll never stop loving Anna.'

'And anyone who loved you would understand that,' Jenny said. 'Because love doesn't make boundaries, James. It stretches them.'

'That's a good way of looking at it. And I know I need to make the effort to find someone else. Tilly needs someone permanent in her life. Though, after what happened with Sophie, I think I might be as clueless as your ex, when it comes to...' He winced. 'Sorry. That's both feet in mouth, now. I didn't mean to...well...'

Jenny smiled, reached over the table, and squeezed his hand briefly. 'Nicely floundered,' she said. 'Everyone thinks that four years is enough time for you to have grieved for Anna; you're still young and they think you need to move on and start dating, even if you might not be ready.' She paused. 'How long has it been since you dated?'

'Since I first dated Anna. Which is about...' He calculated swiftly in his head. 'Ten years,' he said. 'What about you? I imagine you get the same pressure. "It's time to move on",' he quoted.

'Maybe a couple more years,' she said. 'We met in our last year at uni. So we were together for ten, eleven years—and I haven't dated since him.'

Maybe, just maybe, they could help each other.

James took a deep breath. 'You and I—we sort of know each other, and sort of don't,' he said.

'We know *of* each other,' she agreed.

'Given how we both feel about Archer, I think we'll become friends. Good friends,' he said. 'And we both know there's something missing in our lives—*someone*, really. We need to sort out a relationship, but we haven't got the time or the space to do it. Or, at least, we can't afford to take any risks, because we're not the only ones we have to consider. I have Tilly, and you have your mum.'

'Exactly,' she said.

He pulled a face. 'This is ridiculous. If you were a client worried sick about your pet, I wouldn't be pussyfooting about. I'd know exactly what to say. Whereas what's about to come out of my mouth might be...' He shook his head. 'I'd better shut up.'

'Say it,' she said, 'and I promise not to be offended.' She grinned, and added, deliberately hamming up her accent, 'I'm a down-to-earth Yorkshirewoman. Think of me as Jam*ie* Herriot.'

The warmth of her humour felt as if she'd wrapped her arms round him and given him a hug. 'You, me and Archer—the three James—well, James and Jamie—Herriots,' he said. And the expression in her eyes told him she meant it. She wasn't going to be offended, even if he was horrendously clumsy. It didn't matter that his social skills were so rusty, you could practically hear them screeching when he opened his mouth. 'What I was thinking... We're both out of practice at dating,' he said. 'Maybe we can practise on each other.'

'Fake dating, you mean? So people get off our case about having a life partner?'

'Real dates,' he said, 'but they're also practice dates,' he said.

'How do you mean?'

'We haven't dated anyone for years and we've forgotten how to do it—actually, if anything, things have moved on since we last dated and we're old-fashioned as well as rusty. We can't be let loose on other people, because we'll make a mess of it. But if we practise on each other, we can help each other correct our mistakes until we're ready to go out and find Mr, Ms or Dr Right. We'll be safe dating each other, because we both know we're not in a position for this to go anywhere other than being friends. And whatever happens between us, we'll stay friends.'

'Practice dating,' she said. 'With someone safe.'

A little voice in the back of his head pointed out that Jenny might not actually be as safe as he thought she was, but he silenced it. 'It's not going to affect us working together, because we're not romantically involved and we're both professionals. And we won't take offence when either of us points out what the other's doing wrong.'

Dating—but safe.

And hadn't Tamsin been right about her needing some no-strings fun?

On the one hand, it was the perfect solution.

On the other, there was the fact that James Madden's smile made her stomach flip in a way that hadn't happened to her for years. There was a chance that she could lose her heart to him—whereas he might not lose his heart to her in return. Dating him might be a really bad idea.

'You're asking me to date you,' she said. 'Practice date, but still dating. You've been back in the village a week, James. We hadn't seen each other for years before you walked into the practice yesterday. We sort of know each other, in the way that everyone in a village like ours knows everyone else—but at the same time we don't know each other, really.'

'We went to school together. OK, we were in different years, but we have a connection through Archer,' he said. 'And the bits we don't know about each other will help us, because it means it'll be like dating someone we've never met before and need to get to know.'

'So the idea is to practise dating, and when we think we're ready to let ourselves loose on the world I'll help you find a mum for Tilly, and you'll help me to find someone who'll understand I want to look after Mum,' she said.

'And, best of all, in the meantime it'll stop people nagging us about finding a partner,' he said. 'Plus it'll protect us both from anyone who wants to make a move before we're ready.'

Like his former nanny. 'You're right,' she said. 'What just came out of your mouth was something that would floor a lot of women.'

He winced. 'OK. We've established that not only do I put both feet in my mouth, but they also go in right up to the knee. Maybe I need to pin little bells to my jeans, just above my knee.'

The idea was whimsical enough to make her laugh. 'I'm not quite sure that'd be your best fashion move.'

He looked relieved that she wasn't offended. 'Please just forget I said anything, Jenny. I don't want to wreck our friendship, or our relationship at work.'

'Actually, you made some good points,' she said. 'We could both do with some safe, no-strings dating. Practising on someone who isn't going to get the wrong idea or be offended, because we've been open with each other right from the start. And it'll stop all the well-meaning comments that drive me crackers.'

His eyes widened. 'Are you saying you'll do it, Jenny?'

She smiled. 'Yes.' She held her hand out to him to shake on the deal.

And then she kind of wished she hadn't when he took her hand and every nerve-end in her skin seemed to zing at his touch.

'To honesty,' he said, 'and practising.'

'To honesty and practising,' she echoed. She glanced at her watch. 'We need to get back to the surgery.'

'Of course.' James stacked their plates and mugs. 'I'll just take these back in.'

Jenny liked his thoughtfulness; a lot of people would simply have left the crockery for the staff to collect. 'I'll come with you and say goodbye to Sally.'

And weird how it felt like being on the same team.

CHAPTER THREE

HAD HE DONE the right thing? James wondered. He didn't get a chance to see Jenny between the end of surgery and when he had to leave to pick up Tilly from nursery; then he was distracted by his daughter chattering about her day and the new friend she'd just made. By the time he'd washed up the dinner things, given Tilly her bath and gone through the bedtime story routine, and caught up with his parents, it felt too late even to text Jenny.

But she hadn't texted him, either, so hopefully that meant she wasn't having second thoughts.

She texted him on Thursday morning.

Have a nice day. I'm taking Mum for a look round the market in Burnborough and then lunch out. J.

Burnborough was the next village to Burndale; like most of the other villages in their dale, it had a market square in the centre of the village, flanked on three sides by three-storey honey-coloured stone townhouses with white sash windows and on the fourth side by the parish church. The weekly market supplemented what was usually available from the baker, the butcher, the greengrocer and the general store, and was also a good excuse for the villagers to meet up and catch up in the tea shop or the village pub, depending on whether they wanted cake and coffee or a pie and a pint.

Clearly Jenny was hoping that the outing would give her mum a boost.

He texted back.

You have a nice day, too.

And then, on impulse, he added:

Are you and your mum free on Saturday? Might be nice to go out somewhere with Tilly.

Jenny would want to spend her time off-duty with her mum, the way he'd spend his time off-duty with his daughter.

Are you sure that's a good idea? Tilly's had a lot of upheaval—the temp nannies, and I'm not being judgy or blaming you—plus moving here. Is it fair to let her meet me, knowing we're not really dating each other?

He thought about it. And then he thought again.

We're friends, and that's not going to change after the dating lessons. Why wouldn't my daughter meet my friends—just as your mum meets yours?

It was a while before she replied.

OK, you have a point. In that case, that would be lovely. Where do you want to go?

You know what's around here better than I do. Think of somewhere you'd like to go. Off to surgery now.

Was it really that easy to set up a date? Then again, this wasn't like trying to think of somewhere that would impress his date. Somewhere with fabulous food, or a show where tickets were hard to come by, or some cultured kind of exhibition. This was an outing that could be anything from a picnic in the Dales to going on a steam train. And they weren't going on their own: they'd have her mum and his daughter with them.

Which meant that this wasn't even the sort of date where they'd be able to hold hands—and he knew deep down that he'd suggested it precisely for that reason, because he wasn't sure if he was ready to hold hands with someone.

But, if he was going to work up to finding a mum for Tilly, he had to start somewhere. This 'date' with Jenny was the first baby step towards it.

On Friday, James was surprised to see Jenny in the waiting room with a cat carrier on her lap. He knew she wasn't on shift, so it had to be something to do with her mum's cat—unless she was helping out a neighbour. Jenny was just the sort to offer help, despite her own life being packed. She had a kind heart. A huge heart. 'What's happened?' he asked.

'Sooty must've got into a fight last night. When I was going to feed him this morning, I could see his ear was torn, and although I cleaned it at home his ear's in a bit of a mess,' she said. 'If you or Archer don't mind doing the anaesthetic, I can stitch him up myself.'

'You're off duty. Archer and I will do it,' he said.

'I'll be on anaesthetic if you do the stitching, James,' Archer said, joining them in the waiting room and overhearing the conversation. 'I assume Sooty's had nothing to eat since last night?'

'Nothing we've fed him, because when I saw the state of his ear I thought I'd better make him skip his breakfast,' Jenny said. 'Though I can't say what he might have scoffed outside the house.'

'We'll sort him out and let you know as soon as he's round from the anaesthetic and ready to be picked up,' James said. 'I'll ring you. Or, actually, I can drop him in on my way home, if you don't mind Tilly being with me—though be warned that she'll want to make a fuss of him and ask a million questions.'

'Thanks—that'd be great. It'll mean I don't have to ask Sheila next door to come and sit with Mum again while I pick him up,' Jenny said, looking grateful. 'By the way, James, you asked me if I had any ideas of something local that Tilly might like to do at the weekend.'

This was obviously her way of suggesting where they could go on their date, but without letting anyone in the waiting room have a clue what was really being said. Clever, James thought. They'd let it leak out…but not quite yet.

'Maybe she'd like to visit Campbell's Children's Farm?'

'That sounds wonderful,' James said.

'Tilly will love cuddling the bunnies,' Archer said. 'And the guinea pigs—Milly, Molly and Moo.'

'How do you know the names of the guinea pigs?' Jenny asked.

Archer's ears went pink at the tips. 'Halley brought them in for their annual check-up, last week. She's…um…looking after her mum and helping with the farm until Sylvie's hip heals.'

Since when did his best friend go all embarrassed and shy? James vaguely remembered Archer having a crush on Halley Campbell at school, but as far as he knew Archer had never actually done anything about it.

Or, if Halley was back in the village, was this maybe Archer's chance to move on from the sadness of losing Amy?

Though he hated people gossiping about him and trying to fix him up with someone who'd heal his own heartache, so he wasn't going to do that to his best friend.

'Guinea pig cuddling it is,' James said. 'I'll give you a ring when Sooty's round, and I'll bring him back to you on my way home.'

'Thank you.' Jenny gave him a rueful smile. 'I feel guilty leaving him. But I feel guilty about leaving Mum, too, and I didn't want to drag her out with me. Her mobility's not great, this morning.'

'Go home,' James said, taking the carrier from her. 'Sooty will be fine with us.'

'She loves that cat as much as her mum does,' Archer said, when Jenny had left.

James nodded. 'And it's hard, caring for someone vulnerable on your own.'

'You'd know all about that,' Archer said.

'I've got it easy, right now, while I'm staying with Mum. It's still a couple of weeks until we can move into the cottage,' James said. 'So Halley's caring for her mum, too?'

'Until Sylvie's properly back on her feet, yes.'

Archer's expression told James he really didn't want to discuss it further, so James decided to give his friend space and shut up. Between them, they worked their way through the morning's waiting room; once everyone had been seen, they turned their attention to the animals who needed surgery.

Sooty's ear was ragged, but Jenny had cleaned it well, and James stitched it up and administered antibiotics before fitting a collar to make sure that Sooty couldn't take the stitches out with a paw. It would mean Jenny would have to feed him by hand, or take the collar off and then make sure she put it back on again straight after he'd eaten, but better that than having to bring him in to be restitched.

'Well, little man,' he said, making a fuss of the woozy cat once Archer had reversed anaesthetic. 'You'll be fine. Just try and stay out of fights in future, hmm?'

He called Jenny. 'You can tell your mum that Sooty's round from the anaesthetic and he's fine, if a bit sorry for himself. He's had a drink and a little bit to eat. We've stitched his ear and put on a collar so he can't take the stitches out. But you know the drill.'

'Yes. He might have a cough for the rest of the day because of the intubation, and I need to give him antibiotics and pain relief,' Jenny said. 'Thank you, James. Mum will be so relieved that he's OK.'

'See you later,' James said.

And how weird it was that he found himself looking forward to seeing her again.

This was practice dating, not the real thing, he reminded himself.

When he picked Tilly up from nursery, she was delighted to discover they were on a rescue mission and delivering Sooty back to Jenny and her mum. 'Can I cuddle him?'

'You'll need to ask Jenny,' he said. 'And he might still be feeling poorly after his operation and not want a fuss.'

'Did you make him better, Daddy?'

'I did. His ear was poorly and I had to stitch it.'

'I could help you put a bandage on,' she said. 'Except my scrubs, hat and vet bag are at Granny's.'

James had to suppress a grin. Tilly loved the vet play kit that his mother had bought her—including bright pink scrubs—and regularly bandaged all her soft toys and took their temperatures. When his parents' elderly Labrador, Treacle, had been alive, he'd been patient and not minded her bandaging his paw and his tail, too. 'Maybe another time,' he said.

'And he needs flowers if he's poorly, to help make him better,' Tilly added.

James didn't have the heart to tell her that cats didn't need flowers. And, given that Betty had probably worried about Sooty all day, it might be nice to take flowers to her. He'd find a way to persuade his daughter. 'We'll stop at the greengrocer's and see if they have any flowers,' he said.

They made it into the shop literally a minute before closing time.

'I'd like some flowers, please,' he said.

'Pink ones, please,' Tilly added, 'like those ones.' She pointed to the stocks set in a large bucket of water.

'Are these for your grandma?' Mel, who'd owned the shop from as far back as James could remember, asked Tilly.

'No, they're for Sooty. He's poorly,' Tilly said.

'Jenny's mum's cat. I'm dropping him back to her on the way home,' James explained. 'Tilly, I think maybe Mrs Braithwaite would like these flowers a bit more than Sooty would.'

'Is she poorly, too?' Tilly asked.

Out of the mouths of babes, James thought, exchanging a glance with Mel. 'She's been a bit sad today because Sooty's poorly,' he explained.

'Oh. Then we'll give the flowers to her. And you have to buy some flowers for grandma, too, or it isn't fair,' Tilly said.

'That'll be two bunches of stocks, then,' James said resignedly.

Mel grinned. 'If you want a job selling flowers when you grow up, lass, you come and see me.'

Tilly shook her head. 'I'm going to make poorly animals better when I grow up, like Daddy,' she announced.

She chattered about her day at nursery all the way to Jenny's house, and skipped down the path holding his hand and clutching the flowers for Betty.

'Can I press the doorbell?' she asked.

James smiled, hoisting her up with his free arm while holding Sooty's carrier in his other hand, and she pressed the bell.

Jenny opened the door to find an excited nearly four-year-old bouncing on her doorstep in front of James. 'These are for you, Mrs

Braithwaite, to make you feel happy instead of sad,' she said, thrusting the flowers at Jenny.

'Tilly, this is Jenny, who works with me. Mrs Braithwaite is Jenny's mum,' James said gently.

'Oh.' Tilly's huge brown eyes went wide. 'Um… Sorry. I made a mistake.' She turned to James, looking close to tears. 'But if you give someone a present, Daddy, you can't take it back.'

'You can take this present back,' Jenny said, bending down to Tilly's height. 'It'll be our secret that you gave the flowers to me by mistake. Plus these will make my mum very happy. She'll smile, and that'll be a special present for me.'

'Thank you,' Tilly said, taking the flowers back and looking relieved. 'Daddy says Sooty might feel too poorly to be cuddled, but I could tell him a story to make him feel better. I know one from nursery about mice. And I'll bring my scrubs and my vet bag when we come next time, so I can check his temperature and bandage his ear.'

James had warned her that Tilly could be a chatterbox, but Jenny had half expected the little girl to go shy on her, as it was the first time they'd met. Instead, Tilly was vibrant and sunny—and utterly adorable, with that mop of dark curls. Anna, her mother, must've been stunning, Jenny thought, if Tilly took after her. Though Tilly definitely had James's smile.

'Do you want to be a vet like Daddy, when you grow up?' Jenny asked.

'And make them better when they're poorly, like Daddy made Sooty better,' Tilly said, nodding seriously. 'Daddy's scrubs are green, but I like mine better because they're pink.'

Jenny could imagine the little girl dressed in pink scrubs, carrying a veterinary bag, and the vision was delightful. 'Come in,' she said. 'Then we can let Sooty out of his carrier and you can meet him properly, and my mum.'

'Yay!' Tilly said, and skipped indoors.

Sorry, James mouthed.

'Don't be—she's *lovely*,' Jenny said quietly.

She took the cat carrier from him, and led Tilly into the sitting room. 'Mum, you might remember James Madden from school? He's come to work with Archer and me at Burndale Veterinary Surgery, and he stitched Sooty's ear this morning.'

'I remember young James,' Betty said, even though Jenny suspected maybe she didn't. 'Thank you for helping Sooty, James.'

Jenny braced herself for James looking awkward or with his face full of pity, but instead he smiled, leaned forward and kissed Betty on the cheek. 'Lovely to see you again, Mrs Braithwaite. This is my daughter, Tilly.'

'Hello, Tilly,' Betty said.

'Hello, Mrs Braithwaite. We buyed you some flowers. Daddy said you were sad because Sooty has a poorly ear.' Tilly held the flowers out.

'That's very kind of you, young lady. What a pretty colour.' Betty took the flowers gently from her. 'Thank you very much.'

'Pink's my favourite colour. I choosed them,' Tilly said.

Jenny hid a grin. Given that Tilly was dressed top to toe in pink, including her shoes, it was fairly obvious how much the little girl loved pink.

'I can tell Sooty a story to make him feel better,' Tilly said. 'About dancing mice.'

'I'm sure he'd enjoy that,' Betty said.

So would Jenny. She'd loved reading stories to her niece and nephew, when they were small. She'd forgotten how much fun children could be when they were nearly four. 'I'll put the kettle on—if you have time, James?'

'I'd love a cup of tea, thanks,' James said.

'What about you, Tilly? What would you like to drink?'

'Orange juice, please,' Tilly said.

Jenny angled herself so Tilly couldn't see her face, and mouthed to James, *Can I give her a cookie?*

James nodded, and she smiled back in acknowledgement before heading to the kitchen.

When Jenny came back with a tray of tea and orange juice and a plate of choc-chip cookies, James was sitting on the sofa next to her mother's chair, Tilly was cross-legged on the floor next to Sooty, who was curled up in his basket with the cat carrier next to him, and James and Betty were listening intently as Tilly told the sleeping cat a complicated story about dancing mice.

'The end,' Tilly announced, and James and Betty clapped.

In return, Tilly gave them all a beaming smile.

'Thank you for the drink, Miss Braithwaite,' she said politely when Jenny handed her a beaker of orange juice.

'You're very welcome. And call me Jenny,' Jenny said.

'I'm Betty,' her mother said, not to be outdone. Tilly entertained them by telling them about the painting she'd done and the games she'd played at nursery that day, and sang them a song. 'Sooty will like it, because it's all about fishes,' she said.

What Jenny noticed most was how gentle and sweet James was with his daughter—and with her mother, treating her as a normal person rather than a fragile elderly patient with dementia. It was so refreshing, having someone talk to Betty directly, rather than addressing their words awkwardly via Jenny. And she noted, too, that her mother responded to him. It was lovely seeing her mum blossom.

James had a point about them being friends, and staying friends after their dating lessons thing had finished; they'd be able to enrich the lives of her mum and his daughter with that friendship.

And she wasn't going to listen to that tiny voice in the back of her head asking how she'd feel afterwards, if she saw James out on a date with someone else. Because it wasn't relevant. The dating stuff wasn't real.

'We need to go home now, Tilly, because Granny's making tea for us and it's rude to be late,' James said.

Tilly nodded. 'Thank you for having me,'

she said to Jenny. 'And thank you for the juice and cookie.'

'My pleasure, sweetie,' Jenny said, charmed by Tilly's perfect manners.

'Can I come back and tell Sooty another story?' Tilly asked Betty. 'Please,' she added swiftly.

'I'm sure he'd like that. I certainly would,' Betty said.

'Tomorrow?' Tilly asked. 'Daddy doesn't have to work tomorrow and I don't go to nursery on Saturday.'

'I was thinking of taking you out tomorrow,' James said. 'To see some guinea pigs at Campbell's Children's Farm. Maybe Betty and Jenny would like to come with us.'

'And then we can come back here and I can tell Sooty a story?'

James glanced at Jenny, who nodded. 'That's a great idea. He might be feeling a little bit better tomorrow and would listen to you properly.'

'I'd like a kitten,' Tilly said thoughtfully. 'A white one called Twinkle. *And* a puppy called Sir Woofalot.'

Jenny had to suppress a grin at the names.

'We can't have a puppy or a kitten at the moment, darling. Not until we've got our own place and settled in,' James said. 'Now, say goodbye to Betty and Jenny.'

'Bye-bye. See you tomorrow,' Tilly said, blowing them both a kiss and waving madly as James ushered her out of the living room.

Jenny saw them to the front door. 'What time do you need us to be ready, tomorrow?'

'About ten?' James suggested. 'I'll pick you up.'

'Perhaps I'd better pick you up, as Mum's wheelchair fits in my car.'

'It'll fit in mine, too,' James said, 'so I'll collect you both. If you think of anything else I need to know before tomorrow, text me.'

'Thanks for bringing Mum flowers. They really brightened her day—almost as much as Tilly did.'

He looked pleased. 'Good. See you tomorrow.'

For a moment, she thought he might kiss her cheek, and her knees felt as if they'd just turned to jelly.

But instead he smiled and hauled Tilly onto his shoulders, to her delighted giggle, setting her down again by his car so he could strap her into her car seat. They both waved madly to her as they drove off, and Jenny waved back before going back to join her mum.

'It's lovely to have little ones round,' Betty said. 'And she's such a chatterbox. Just like you, at that age.' She smiled. 'And James. He's a nice young man—he's kind, and he makes time for people.'

Jenny knew exactly what her mum wasn't saying. That James was the complete opposite of Simon. A family man.

'Well, we'll be spending tomorrow with them,' she said brightly. 'It'll be nice to have a day out.'

On Saturday morning, James texted Jenny to check that she and Betty were still able to go to the children's farm, then picked them up.

'I wasn't sure if it'd be easier for your mum in the front or the back,' he said, 'but Tilly's in the back, to make the choice easy for her.'

'Front, please,' Jenny said. 'Mum likes to walk a bit, although she can't walk very fast—and it's good for her, giving her confidence that she isn't going to fall. The chair's really just a precaution, for when she gets tired.'

'Got it,' James said.

Betty walked very slowly, and gripped a cane to help her keep her balance; James held the car door for her and helped her into the passenger seat, then put the lightweight wheelchair into the boot of the car.

Jenny climbed into the back with Tilly, who chattered all the way to the farm—and was almost beside herself with glee at the idea of being up close with the animals and being allowed to feed them. Her voice got louder and louder, the nearer they got to the farm.

'Remember, Tilly, you need to use your indoor voice at the farm,' James said as he parked the car.

'So the guinea pigs don't get scared,' she said, nodding solemnly.

'That's right,' he said, smiling. 'Good girl.'

She skipped along beside him happily, and he tried to keep their pace the same as Betty's. After a chat with Halley and Sylvie—and the all-important purchase of a bag of feed—they went to see the animals.

Tilly thoroughly enjoyed cuddling the guinea pigs and was thrilled to be allowed to brush one of the rabbits.

'He's happy,' she said, 'because his nose is all twitchy.'

Jenny caught his eye and grinned. 'You're absolutely right, Tilly. Daddy's obviously been training you so you know if a bunny's nose doesn't twitch, that tells you he might be poorly or not feeling very happy.'

'Happy bunnies hop a lot, too,' Tilly said. 'I'm happy, but you have to be really gentle with bunnies so I'm not going to hop in here, in case I scare them.'

She's adorable, Jenny mouthed at James over the top of Tilly's head.

Yes. She was. And it warmed him all the way through that Jenny could see that, too.

Halfway round the farm, Betty admitted defeat and sank gratefully into the wheelchair. James pushed her chair along the path, while Tilly held Jenny's hand and chattered to her about all the animals they passed.

How Anna would've loved this, James thought, and it put a lump in his throat. How much his wife was missing out on. How much *Tilly* was missing out on.

When they reached the pygmy goats, Tilly asked Betty to help her feed them. James helped Betty out of the chair, and together Betty and Tilly fed the goats, Betty encouraging the little girl to hold her hand flat so the goats could nibble the feed pellets from her hand.

'That's so lovely to see,' Jenny whispered, taking James's hand briefly and squeezing it.

'Mum really feels it that she doesn't see the grandchildren very much—they're heading into their teens so they don't really have the patience to spend time with her, and we're lucky if my brother visits once a month.'

'Yes.'

Obviously Jenny heard the slight wobble in his voice, because she asked quietly, 'Are you OK, James?'

'Yes,' he said. 'And no,' he admitted, a few moments later, knowing it was unfair to push her away when none of this was her fault. They were friends, and she understood his situation a little more than most people because her own was so similar. 'I guess it's all a bit…' He paused, searching for the right word. 'Bittersweet. As you say, it's lovely to see Tilly and your mum making friends with each other and enjoying feeding the goats. But this is the sort of thing I always imagined doing with Anna, when she was pregnant. I thought we'd go to one of these places with our children, watch the joy on their faces when the goats or lambs or whatever ate feed from their hands. And it makes me realise how many things we didn't get the time to share. How much she's missed out on—and Tilly, too.'

'It wasn't your fault that Anna died. You

admitted it yourself. It wasn't anyone's fault. Nobody could be expected to guess that she'd have an amniotic fluid embolism, because it's a really rare complication,' Jenny said softly.

He knew. He'd looked up the stats. Anna had simply been unlucky.

And how hard it was to get past that. To move on.

'Think of it another way. You can still do things with Tilly, and you can talk to her about her mum. You can share things with her. That's important,' she said.

He nodded, unable right then to reply.

'After I split up with Simon—even though it was the right thing for both of us, and there wasn't any real acrimony—I spent a while thinking about all the might-have-beens,' Jenny said. 'All the things we could've done differently. We could've had a family, or persuaded his boss to come to an arrangement with London so he could've worked some of the time in London and some of the time in Leeds. Or we could even have moved to Manchester, with Mum, so we'd be nearer my brother and she could see more of the grandchildren while Simon had the challenge he needed in his job. And it just made me miserable, thinking of all the things we didn't do.'

She took a deep breath. 'It's taken me a while to work it out, but I learned that living in the present and making the most of life made me feel a lot happier.'

James looked at her. Clearly not having children was something she regretted, despite telling him that she'd come to terms with not having a family. And, given the way she'd been with Tilly earlier, James rather thought Jenny would have made a great mum. That part of Jenny's life hadn't worked out the way she might've wanted it to, but she'd done well in her career and she was clearly very close to her mum.

Living in the present. Making the most of life.

That was what he needed to do, now. For his own sake as well as Tilly's.

And move on.

'Thank you,' he said. 'For understanding. And for showing me a different way to look at things.' This time, he was the one to take her hand and squeeze it. 'You're right. It doesn't mean I have to put all my memories of Anna in a box, but I do need to live in the here and now instead of dwelling on the might-have-beens—otherwise, I'll end up realising I've missed things I didn't want to miss.'

'You'll be fine,' she said. 'And so will Tilly.'

Jenny's belief in him was humbling. And he really didn't want to let her hand go. He actually *liked* holding her hand. He liked the warmth of her fingers entwined with his, the silky softness of her skin. After all, this was supposed to be a practice date, of sorts. But he realised he'd gone about it completely the wrong way—or maybe he'd done it so he wouldn't have to make the effort to move on, using Tilly and Betty as an excuse. Right now, he didn't want to have to explain to Tilly why he was holding Jenny's hand, any more than he guessed Jenny wanted to explain it to Betty.

Next time, he'd make the date just for the two of them.

He smiled at her—hoping his expression said more than the words he couldn't quite scramble together—and loosened her hand.

When Tilly had run out of animals to cuddle or feed, James suggested that maybe they could head to the next village for lunch.

'Will they have fish fingers, Daddy?' Tilly asked.

'If they don't,' he promised, 'then I'll make you some tonight.'

He enjoyed driving through the dales, taking a narrow country road with a drystone wall either side that had weathered to a dark grey and was covered in golden moss. There were fields of wheat on either side, interspersed with green pasture where fluffy white sheep with black faces were grazing.

'Look, Jenny! There are lambs!' he heard Tilly squeak from the back.

And then he had to stop as a ewe wandered out into the middle of the road, a lamb trotting along beside her.

'Traffic jam,' he said, and put his hazard lights on so anyone coming behind him would realise that he'd had to stop.

They waited while the ewe walked down the middle of the road, the lamb's tail wagging happily as it walked beside its mum.

'I'm hungry,' Tilly said forlornly.

'I know, sweetheart, but we have to wait for the sheep to move out of the road,' James said. 'We can't rush them. It'll worry them, and that's not kind.'

'Do you know any songs about lambs or sheep, Tilly?' Jenny asked.

It was the perfect distraction, because Tilly loved singing. James was pretty sure he knew exactly what was coming, and just as he'd expected he heard his daughter start singing

'Baa Baa, Black Sheep.' Though, to his surprise, both Jenny and Betty joined in.

'I know another song about sheep,' Betty said. '"Little Bo-Peep".'

'I don't know that one,' Tilly said.

'I'll teach you.' Betty began to sing the nursery song—but then she stalled halfway through. 'Leave them alone, and...'

James could see her shaking her head, out of the corner of his eyes, clearly distressed that the words had slipped away. 'And they'll come home,' he sang, hoping the prompt would help her.

'Wagging their tails behind them,' Betty finished. He gave her a sideways glance and noticed how relieved she looked. He'd just bet Jenny was relieved, too.

'That's a lovely song,' Tilly said.

'And the lamb in front of us is wagging its tail,' James said. 'They're back on the side of the road. Watch its tail as we go past.'

He drove very slowly and carefully past the sheep, then picked up a little more speed when the sheep were safely behind them. Once Tilly got hungry, she started getting grumpy, and he wanted to avoid that.

As if Jenny realised that distraction was still required, she said, 'I know a song about sheep and lots of other animals. Can you guess what it is, Tilly?'

'No,' Tilly said, and there was a touch of plaintiveness in her voice.

'I can,' Betty said, and launched into 'Old MacDonald'.

This time, James found himself joining in with the three of them.

And there was nothing nicer than driving through such beautiful scenery, the verges of the roads frothy with Queen Anne's lace and the odd sprinkle of scarlet poppies and purple meadow cranesbill, while singing nursery songs together.

This felt like being a family. The family he'd envisioned until Anna had been cruelly taken from them.

Except he wasn't going to live in the might-have-beens. He was going to take Jenny's advice and live in the now.

Finally they made it through the winding road to the next village. Like most of the villages in this part of the Dales, the houses were built from honey-coloured stone and slate roofs, with large sash windows; they stood cheek by jowl around the marketplace. James parked, put some money in the honesty box, and they found a table in the café in the square.

To his relief, the waitress was able to sort out some fish fingers and crispy fries with ketchup for Tilly, while he, Jenny and Betty all plumped for a bacon sandwich served with chunky chips and home-made coleslaw.

Tilly ate every scrap, and Jenny gently wiped the tomato ketchup from the little girl's face with a paper napkin.

'That was crump-shuss,' Tilly announced when the waitress came over. 'Thank you!'

'You're welcome, lass,' the waitress said. She smiled at Jenny. 'Your daughter has lovely manners.'

'Jenny's not my mummy,' Tilly said.

James winced inwardly. That kind of flat rejection was one of the reasons he hadn't tried dating yet.

'Jenny's my friend,' Tilly continued. 'She works with my daddy. They make poorly animals better. My mummy's in heaven.'

'Well, I'm sure your mummy's glad you have a nice friend,' the waitress said.

'I agree—and I'm glad, too,' James said. He risked a glance at Jenny, who was smiling.

'Me, three,' Jenny said. 'Mum?'

'Me, four,' Betty said.

Tilly worked it out. 'That's me, five—except I'm not, 'cos I'm nearly four and it's my birthday next month!'

Everyone laughed, and the awkward moment was dispersed, to James's relief.

Tilly dropped off to sleep in the car on the way back to Burndale, and didn't wake when James took Jenny and Betty back to their cottage.

'Thank you for today,' Betty said, kissing his cheek. 'Your little girl is such a sweetheart. And she'll be so disappointed not to have told Sooty a story. Bring her any time.'

'Thank you,' James said with a smile.

A glance over his shoulder reassured him that his daughter was still sound asleep.

'Thank you for coming with us,' he said to Jenny.

She smiled. 'So how would you rate it as a date?'

'Apart from when I went all mopey on you at the farm, and that moment in the café when Tilly said…' He grimaced, not wanting to repeat it and rub it in.

Jenny smiled. 'It's fine. She didn't mean it in a horrible way. And she likes me enough to call me her friend. That's a good thing.' She paused. 'So. Verdict?'

'I enjoyed myself,' James said. 'Actually, it's been the perfect afternoon. I can't remember the last time I relaxed so much—or enjoyed myself so much.' Since Anna's death, though he wasn't going to be tactless enough to say so. And it also made him feel the tiniest bit disloyal towards Anna. 'How about you? Have you had a nice day?'

'I enjoyed myself, too,' she said. 'I think we can say that we both managed a super-safe date-that-isn't-a-date.'

'I would shake on that,' James said, 'but I don't think you're supposed to shake hands with your date. Though I'm out of touch with dating etiquette. Do I ask permission to kiss your cheek?'

'Do you want to kiss my cheek?' she asked.

He held her gaze, enjoying the hint of mischief in those stunning blue eyes. 'What would you do if I said yes?'

The glint in her eyes deepened; she stood on tiptoe, rested her hands on James's shoulders and kissed his cheek. 'That's what I'd do,' she said.

All the nerve-endings in his skin seemed to have come to life in the place where she'd kissed him, and it flummoxed him to the point where he dared not kiss her cheek in case the feel of her skin against his mouth wiped every single word out of his head. 'Well,' he said gruffly. 'That's settled, then.'

'Better get little one home,' she said. 'See you at work on Monday.'

'See you on Monday,' he echoed.

And, even though it had been sunny all day, oddly her smile made him feel as if the sun had just come out again after a long, cold winter.

CHAPTER FOUR

ON SUNDAY MORNING, James was called out to treat a couple of calves with severe diarrhoea, a condition known as scouring.

The four calves in the isolation pen all had slightly sunken eyes, showing they were dehydrated.

'Have they been off their feed?' James asked.

'Aye, and the scour's bright yellow,' Reuben Farley, the farmer, confirmed.

'How old are they?' James asked.

Reuben sighed. 'Two weeks. It's just these four affected, right now, but I'm keeping a close eye on the rest. The scouring started yesterday, and they're getting sicker. We vaccinated the cows before calving, and we made sure the calves had as much colostrum as they could straight after they were born, so they get as much protection as possible against rotavirus, coronavirus and E. coli, and we're very careful with hygiene.'

'Scouring in most calves of this age often has mixed causes, but as you've vaccinated the cows I think it's most likely cryptosporidium,' James said. Cryptosporidium was a protozoal organism, and eggs passed in the faeces of infected animals could survive for months. Because it wasn't a bacteria, antibiotics wouldn't help to treat the infection, and there were no protective antibodies for cryptosporidium in a cow's colostrum. All he could do was give medication if the lab tests showed that the calves were affected. 'I brought some sample pots with me, so we can check the scour samples at the lab to see what's causing the problem. Then I'll be able to sort out the right medication.'

'Right you are,' Reuben said.

'Are they bucket-fed or suckling?' James asked.

'Bucket-fed.'

'OK. The main thing is rehydrating them while we're waiting for the test results. I assume you already have electrolyte solution?'

'Aye, lad.'

'Good. Start the calves on them now, and

I'd advise doing it half an hour before their milk feed.'

'You don't want me to take them off the milk for a day or two, like I usually do?'

James shook his head. 'The milk will help heal their intestines. Don't dilute the milk with the electrolytes, because it'll affect clotting. Obviously you know they need twice as much fluid as usual, to replace what they've lost. I'd suggest frequent small feeds rather than three big ones a day. I'll take the samples straight to the lab, so we should know what's causing the scouring within later this afternoon and I'll bring the medication over.' He gave Reuben a wry smile. Given that he was in his late fifties, Reuben would've seen all this many times before, and he'd know the routine. 'I don't need to tell you how easily the infection can spread.'

'Aye, lad.' Reuben looked grim. 'I know it can pass to humans, so I'll make everyone use gloves and change them between handling the calves, wash their hands thoroughly, change their clothes and disinfect their boots after they've been in this area.'

'Great.' James pulled his rubber boots on and disinfected them before gloving up. 'It's best to get samples fresh from the calves rather than the floor.'

'Shall we split it and do two calves each?' Reuben suggested.

'Two each,' James agreed. Even though he was wearing a boiler suit over his jeans and T-shirt, he'd shower and change his clothes after he'd taken the samples to the lab.

Taking samples of bright yellow liquid faeces from the calves was one of the least glamorous parts of James's job, but it was completely necessary to find out what exactly was causing the scouring so he could recommend the right treatment. He disinfected his boots again once they'd taken the samples and left the pen, and at his car he stripped off the boiler suit and put it in a bag for washing. He accepted Reuben's offer of scrubbing his hands at the farm and a cup of tea, and messaged Archer and Jenny to keep them in the loop. He dropped off the samples to the lab in Richmond, then drove back to Burndale.

The journey was glorious: winding, gentle rolling hills, punctuated with drystone walls and the occasional slate-roofed stone farmhouse. You could see the undulating fields for miles at the top of the dale, bright green pasture with clusters of tress and white dots of grazing sheep across the other side of the valley. At the bottom, a sinuous river carved its way through, looking silver in the sunlight.

It was perfect.

And it was only now that James realised how hard it had been for him to breathe in London. He'd grown used to the city, for Anna's sake, but here in the open countryside was where he realised he really belonged.

Though it wasn't just the beauty of the Yorkshire Dales that drew him.

If he was to be honest with himself, Jenny was a big part of it, too.

But she didn't want a relationship right now; that was the whole reason why she'd agreed to help him to practise dating. It wouldn't go any further between them than friendship, and wouldn't make unfair demands on her time. Much as he liked her—and liked the way she was with his daughter—he needed to respect her situation.

Later that day, the lab texted him with the results, confirming cryptosporidium.

'Mum, would you mind looking after Tilly while I take some medication to one of my farmers?' James asked.

'You're going to a farm?' Tilly's eyes were huge with hope. 'Can I come with you, Daddy?'

James was about to say no: but, then again, she wasn't going to be touching the calves. Plus he liked having his daughter with him. 'As long as you hold my hand all the time we're on the farm,' he said, 'and you mustn't touch the calves or go close, because they're poorly.'

He picked up the medication from the surgery, then drove them out to Reuben's farm and introduced Reuben to Tilly. 'Reuben, this is my assistant—also known as my daughter, Tilly,' he said. 'She wants to be a vet when she grows up. Tilly, this is Mr Farley.'

'Hello,' Tilly said shyly.

'Hello, lass. Always good to follow in your father's footsteps,' Reuben said.

'I promise I won't touch the calves,' Tilly said, 'because they're poorly. And I'm using my indoor voice so I won't scare them.'

'Good lass,' Reuben said approvingly.

Copying James, she disinfected her wellies and followed Reuben to the calves' pen.

'Give this to the calves daily for the next week,' James told Reuben, handing over the medication, 'and it'll stop the cryptosporidium multiplying. Hopefully the calves will all pick up again in a couple of days. They're looking brighter than they were earlier.'

'The rehydration's already helping,' Reuben said. 'I've got another couple of calves I'm isolating in a separate pen, just in case— they're not scouring right now, but their temperatures are up a bit, they're a bit lethargic and lying around, and they're being a bit fussy with their milk.'

'It sounds like you've caught them at the earliest stage, just before they start scouring,' James agreed. 'I'd start the second lot on the cryptosporidium treatment, too, as a preventative.'

'Right you are, lad.'

'Will they get better, Daddy?' Tilly asked.

'They will,' James said.

'Good.' Tilly beamed.

'Come back to the house with us, lass,' Reuben said. 'You can say hello to Mrs Farley. And you can see our Gem's pups, if you like.'

'Puppies?' Tilly's eyes widened. 'Daddy said we can have a puppy when we move into our new house.'

'Oh, aye?' Reuben smiled. 'Well, most of these ones have new homes lined up already, I'm afraid. And they need to stay with their mum for another month or so.'

James could almost see the wheels turning in his daughter's head, and knew exactly what was coming next. 'Will we have our new house by then, Daddy? Can we have one of Mr Farley's pups?'

'Maybe,' he said.

'It's my birthday next month,' she reminded him.

Yes, and she'd made it very clear what she wanted.

'When I get a puppy, I'm going to call him Sir Woofalot,' she told Reuben.

The farmer grinned. 'Well, now. That's quite a name for a dog.'

'And we're going to have a kitten called Twinkle,' Tilly added.

Reuben's grin broadened as he looked at James. 'Sounds as if you're going to have your hands full.'

As James could've predicted, Tilly fell in love with the litter of springer spaniel puppies, and thoroughly enjoyed sitting on the floor with them while they clambered over her. Though James couldn't resist giving a couple of the pups a cuddle, too.

'She's a bonny lass, your girl,' Susan, Reuben's wife, said. 'Good with animals. Knows how to give them space.'

'Going to be a vet, just like her dad, she says,' Reuben told her. 'After a pup, she is.'

He tipped his head towards the puppies and tapped his nose. 'And it's her birthday next month.'

James groaned. 'When we've moved into the cottage we're renting and settled in, provided the landlord doesn't mind us having pets, maybe we'll look for a pup.'

'You're renting a place from Ben Williams, aren't you? He loves dogs,' Reuben said. 'Can't see it being a problem.'

'The runt of the litter's made himself quite at home on her,' Susan remarked. 'And nobody's booked him, yet.'

'He'd be much happier as a pet than as a working dog,' Reuben said. 'And your lass'd learn a lot from having a pup and training him how to be a good boy. You have a think about it, James. That little one's yours, if you want him. And he can stay with us a bit longer, if you haven't moved by the time the pups are ready to leave their mum.'

'It wouldn't be fair to leave a pup at home on his own all day,' James said, as a last-ditch attempt.

'I'm sure your mum and dad would help you out. I know they miss their Treacle,' Susan said.

That was the thing about living in a village.

Everyone knew everyone—and they knew all the details of everyone else's lives, too.

'Maybe,' James hedged. But he had a feeling that the liver and white springer pup currently asleep on Tilly's lap would end up going home with them in a few weeks. 'Tilly, we need to go home now, love,' he said.

Susan scooped the sleeping pup off Tilly's lap and, reluctantly, Tilly said goodbye to the rest of the puppies and got to her feet. 'Thank you for letting me see the puppies, Mr and Mrs Farley,' she said politely.

'You're very welcome, lass,' Susan said. 'You can come and see them any time your dad's free.'

Tilly beamed. 'Thank you!'

Later that evening, James sent Jenny a text, telling her the sorry tale of how he was close to being talked into letting Tilly have one of the Farleys' pups.

She called him. 'How can you possibly resist a pup?' she asked. 'Those warm, fat little tummies, that lovely popcorn smell when you nuzzle them, those lovely big eyes...'

'Not to mention the puppy breath,' he countered. 'Tiny teeth that feel like needles every time they shred your skin. The joy of getting up in the night and accidentally standing in a puddle of puppy pee.'

She laughed. 'Oh, you *fraud*. I bet you had a cuddle with the pups as well.'

'Yes, I did,' James admitted. 'It's one of the privileges of being a vet. You can cuddle as many puppies and kittens as you like, but you can also give them back.'

The grin was obvious in her voice when she said, 'I have a feeling Sir Woofalot might be coming home with you.'

'Even if I've moved into the cottage by the time the pups are ready to come home, the landlord might not want me to have a pet,' he protested.

'James, anyone who rents a cottage in the Dales to a vet *knows* there will be animals in the house. Besides, Ben Williams loves dogs. I don't think he's going to have a problem if you want a pet.'

He really didn't have a choice with this, did he? 'Tilly wants a kitten called Twinkle and a puppy called Sir Woofalot.' He groaned. 'But I can't leave a pup at home all day.'

'You won't have to,' Jenny said confidently.

'I can't take him to work, either.'

'I know, but your mum bumped into Mum and me in the baker's the other week and she told us how much she misses taking Treacle for walks.' Jenny paused. 'Ask her what she thinks about the pup. I bet she offers to help you out while the pup's still tiny.'

Exactly what Reuben and Susan had said. Was the whole village ganging up on him? 'Maybe,' James said. Wanting to head her off, he changed the subject. 'I was going to ask you: could we have another practice date this week? I thought maybe we could go for a drink one evening. Just you and me.'

'When were you thinking?'

'Mum has her dance fitness class on Tuesday and her book group's on Wednesday,' James said. 'Any other evening, she'll be happy to look after Tilly.'

'How about Thursday?' Jenny suggested. 'Maybe seven, so we can be out for a couple of hours. I'll see if Tamsin can sit with Mum. If she can't, then maybe Friday?'

'That'd be great. Thanks. I'll see you tomorrow at work,' he said.

It turned out that Tamsin was free on Thursday, and James picked Jenny up, as arranged.

They drove to a village that sprawled along the stream at the bottom of the dale. The local pub was ancient, with a stone floor and a huge fireplace, and it had a pretty garden shaded by apple trees. James bought their drinks, and they found a quiet table in the garden, sitting next to each other rather than opposite and watching the bees hum lazily over the lavender flowers in the border.

Now it was just the two of them, James felt weirdly shy.

'What's wrong?' Jenny asked, clearly picking up on his discomfiture.

'It's been so long since I was at the early stages of dating someone, I don't even know how I'm supposed to act,' he said. 'Do I hold your hand? Put my arm round you?'

'That's why we're doing the practising, isn't it?' Jenny asked. 'What do you want to do?'

Kiss her.

Though this was Jenny. His *friend.* He wasn't supposed to be thinking about her like that. 'What do you want me to do?' he countered.

She laughed. 'You can hold my hand, if you like. But mainly talk to me, so I can get to know you.'

'You already know me. You work with me,' he pointed out.

She coughed. 'Practice dating means practising what you'd do on a date. Tell me about your social life—what you enjoy doing.'

Feeling slightly awkward, he laced his fingers through hers. 'Is that OK?'

'It's fine,' she reassured him. 'Relax, James.'

But holding her hand made him feel all flustered and he didn't have a clue what to say next.

'Your social life?' she reminded him gently.

'Right now,' James said ruefully, 'it consists mainly of visits to the playground and the park, learning to do really good different voices when I'm reading bedtime stories, and visits to zoos and sea life centres.'

She grinned. 'Actually, that sounds like fun. I'm rather fond of jellyfish, myself. They're fascinating creatures. It's a few years since I took my niece and nephew to a sea life place, but I remember they had these huge tanks for the jellyfish, under a purple light. I could've watched them for hours.'

'Tilly's favourites are the sharks,' he said. 'The bigger, the better. And the giant rays.'

Jenny shivered. 'Sharks are magnificent to watch, yes; but the rays always scare me. I think it's their mouths. I'm glad we don't have any sea-life centres as clients. The idea of having to treat one, with those huge teeth…'

'They have suction plates, not teeth,' he said. 'So they're not going to hurt you or bite you when you feed them. If anything, their jaws make them more like a cow chewing the cud.'

'Except they're chewing anchovies and shellfish,' Jenny said. 'Which is *not* like chewing grass.'

'Fair point.' He smiled. 'Tilly's fascinated by them. You can guess what I'm planning for her eighth birthday, the first time she'll be old enough to feed them.'

'A VIP ray-feeding trip? She'll love that,' Jenny said. 'But rather her than me!'

'What about you?' he asked. 'What do you do in your social life?'

'Visit gardens,' she said. 'I take Mum to a stately home most weekends, especially the kind of places that have all-terrain paths for wheelchairs in the grounds. And then,' she added with a grin, 'hard though it is, we force ourselves to head for the tea shop and have a pot of tea with scones, jam and cream.'

'What a tough life,' James said, mirroring her light tone. 'Actually, I'm a bit envious. Tilly's not a fan of scones. When we eat out, she wants fish fingers or sausages and *lots* of ketchup.'

'Fish finger sandwiches,' she said, 'are a thing of joy.'

Clearly he didn't look convinced, because she smiled. 'You might like the foodie version. Sourdough bread, with little gem lettuce and sliced plum tomatoes. Mayo on the bread next to the lettuce, tartare sauce on the fish finger side, all served with some crispy sweet potato fries.'

'Actually, that does sound nice,' he said.

'Let's make it a lunch date,' she said. 'Mum likes fish finger sandwiches, too. Tilly can help me put the sandwiches together, and we'll do a mixture of sweet potato and skinny fries so she can try them both.'

'That'd be lovely, but won't that be a lot of work for you?' he asked, mindful that her free time was limited.

'Not with an air fryer,' she said with a wink. 'It's the best labour-saving device ever. Especially on days when I'm working and pick Mum up from the day-care centre on the way home—that and the slow-cooker mean I don't have to spend huge amounts of time in the kitchen sorting out dinner instead of spending time with Mum.' She gave him a rueful smile. 'And if it's a day when Mum's struggling with cutlery, I can do finger foods so she keeps her independence.'

'Sounds as if you're a brilliant organiser,' he said. 'I had to learn the hard way how to organise a home and cook for a child. Anna and I tended to eat out or get takeaways, and if we had friends round for dinner she'd do the cooking and I'd do all the clearing up.'

'At least you shared the work,' she said.

He raised an eyebrow. 'Your ex expected you to do everything?' OK, so she'd said he was a neurosurgeon; but Jenny's job was demanding, too.

'Looking back, I probably should've been a bit less accommodating,' she said. 'But you can't change the past, so it's a bit pointless dwelling on it.'

'True.' He paused. 'So, apart from visiting gardens, what do you like doing?'

'I used to like walking in the Dales, when Dad was alive,' she said. 'But Mum can't manage uneven ground or steep slopes. It's fine. Like I said, we find places with good accessibility. Places where we can potter around without worrying.' She smiled. 'What about you?'

'Live music, theatre, the cinema,' he said.

'Anna and I made a list of all the hidden corners of London and worked our way through it—everything from a candlelight concert in one of the churches through going on a tour of the bits of the Tube that aren't usually open to the public. And we both loved street food.'

'That sounds good,' she said. 'I used to like the cinema, too. There was a fabulous cinema with comfy sofas in Leeds city centre, and a pop-up cinema during the summer in the grounds of Kirkstall Abbey ruins.'

'Maybe we can go to the cinema, some time,' he said. Maybe holding her hand in the dark would be a little bit less unsettling than holding her hand in the daylight.

'Maybe,' she said. 'And it's always lovely walking by the canal or a river. If I'd lived in London, I would definitely have done the Thames Path.'

'Maybe we can do some walks by the canals locally,' he said. 'Hebden Bridge, or Skipton—if it's dry, your mum's wheelchair would cope just fine with the towpath. And if we see narrowboats going through the locks, it'll be interesting for her and for Tilly.'

Jenny nodded. 'That's a nice idea, as long

as you don't mind us taking up time on your weekend.'

'Of course I don't. Tilly likes you,' he said. 'Plus there will be shops selling ice-cream, which just about beats fish fingers for her.'

She laughed, and he noticed how pretty she was when she laughed, with those stunning blue eyes crinkling at the corners.

'Do you miss London?' she asked.

'I've only been back in Burndale for a couple of weeks, so it's probably not quite long enough for me to miss it,' he said. 'Though I admit I miss how everything was on my doorstep—we lived in Hackney, so we were only half an hour away from the centre of the city. Then again, much as I like Hackney Marshes, nothing quite compares to the Yorkshire Dales.'

'It was a bit of a shock to the system when I first came back to Burndale,' she said. 'Going from small animal work to treating farm animals—it felt like being a rookie again.'

'I'm lucky,' he said, 'because I got to do farm animals in London.'

'How?' she asked.

'One of our clients was a children's farm,' he said. 'A bit bigger than Campbell's Children's Farm—there were sheep and pigs, and a couple of cows. Though I admit it's nice coming back and seeing proper herds in the fields again. I missed that.'

'Talking of herds, is there any news on Reuben Farley's calves?'

'They're doing well. The second lot went down with scour the next day, as he suspected, but because we caught them at an earlier stage they haven't been as sick,' James said.

'And Sir Woofalot?' she asked.

'I talked it over with Mum,' he said. 'She's all for it. She thinks it'll be a good way of teaching Tilly responsibility—making sure the pup has plenty of water, proper feeding times and exercise, as well as grooming and teaching some basic obedience.' He wrinkled his nose. 'Actually, she gave Reuben a ring and went over to see the pups while Tilly was at nursery on Monday. It seems there was another pup left in the litter apart from Sir Woofalot. A black and white one.'

'Which is now your mum's?' Jenny asked.

He nodded ruefully. 'I wish I'd realised how much she missed Treacle. I would've suggested her getting another dog sooner.' He glanced at his watch. 'And I guess we need to make a move. We said we'd only be a couple of hours, and we're a good twenty minutes away from Burndale.'

'I've enjoyed this,' Jenny said.

'Me, too,' James said.

In the car, he turned to her. 'If I kiss you goodnight at your place, it's going to fuel rumours, and I'm not quite sure I'm ready for that just yet. So may I kiss you now?'

She smiled, and stroked his cheek. 'Yes.'

He pressed a kiss into her palm, then drew her hand down and leaned over to kiss her. Just lightly, his lips brushing against hers, a whisper of a kiss.

When she slid her other hand round the back of his neck and kissed him back, it felt as if a slow fuse had lit and heat started shimmering through him. For a moment, he was dizzy. He'd forgotten how it felt to kiss someone, the teasing friction that made you want to get closer and closer.

When he finally broke the kiss, he was shaking. Somehow he had to bring back some lightness, so Jenny didn't realise just how much that kiss had affected him. 'Not bad for a practice kiss,' he said.

'Eight out of ten,' she said.

He nearly suggested a second kiss, to see if he could improve his score, but held himself back. This was Jenny. His colleague. His friend. She was supposed to be *safe*, not putting him into a spin.

'Uh-huh,' he said, and drove them back to Burndale.

'Do you want to come in, just to say hello to Mum?' she asked when they arrived at the cottage.

It would be horribly rude not to, James thought. And Jenny had probably told Tamsin the truth about their 'date'; the deputy headteacher wouldn't gossip, in any case. 'Sure,' he said, following her into the cottage.

Betty was sitting in her chair in the living room, and made to get up.

'You don't need to get up for me, Betty,' he said, going over to her and kissing her on the cheek. 'I need to get back to Tilly, but I just wanted to pop in and say hello to you before I go.'

'It's lovely to see you.' Betty smiled at him. 'Did you both have a nice time?'

'Very nice, thank you,' he said. 'We found a lovely pub near the river, with a garden full of apple trees and lavender.' He smiled at Tamsin. 'Hi, Tamsin. Nice to see you. Thanks for that list you gave me—it's very helpful and I've got a couple of playdates arranged for Tilly.'

'Good.' Tamsin gave him an assessing glance.

Remembering that she was Jenny's best friend, he decided to drop her a text to reassure her that he and Jenny were friends, and he'd never do anything to hurt her.

'Would you like to come for lunch on Sunday, James?' Betty asked. 'Tilly can read Sooty a story, and I'll make my apple pie.'

'That'd be lovely. Thank you, I'd like that,' James said. 'Jenny was trying to convince me how nice fish finger sandwiches are.'

'They're lovely, the way my Jenny makes them,' Betty said.

'It's a date. Fish finger sandwiches and apple pie,' James said, and kissed her cheek again. 'I'll sort out the time with Jenny. Bye, Tamsin.'

'I'll see you out,' Jenny said. 'I think you might've made Mum's day,' she said when they were at the front door.

'I like your mum, very much,' James said. 'She was the secretary at school, wasn't she? I remember her being very kind to me in Year Seven when someone tackled me a bit too hard on the sports field and I thought I'd broken my wrist.' He rolled his eyes. 'Luckily it was just a bad sprain, but I appreciated her looking after me while I was waiting for Mum to come and pick me up.'

'You'll have to tell her about that,' Jenny said. Her smile held a tinge of sadness. 'It's far back enough for her to still have a clear memory of it.'

'Hey. You're doing a brilliant job, looking after her. She's safe and she's happy.' On impulse, he leaned forward and kissed the tip of her nose. 'And *you* are amazing. I'll see you Sunday. Text me later to tell me what time to be here.'

Jenny watched him drive away.

Holding hands with James on a practice date was one thing. Kissing him in the car had been quite another; it had thrown her that she'd wanted to respond to him so much. Her cheeky marks-out-of-ten comment had been designed for self-preservation, and thankfully he hadn't noticed that he'd put her in such a spin.

And now this completely unexpected, very sweet demonstration of affection had made her gulp. Hard.

She was really going to have to keep a grip on her emotions. It would be very easy to let herself fall for James Madden—and that would make life way too complicated. For both of them.

CHAPTER FIVE

On Sunday, James and Tilly arrived for lunch.

Tilly handed a painting to Jenny with a huge smile. 'It's Sooty. I made it for you.'

'It's gorgeous,' Jenny said. 'I'll put it on my fridge.'

'I was going to bring wine,' James said, 'but I wasn't sure if your mum likes wine, so I brought these.'

He'd bought locally made cordials from the farm shop just outside Burndale: elder-flower, and a deep ruby-coloured raspberry and lemon, along with a bottle of sparkling water.

'Thank you, James. That's really thought-ful.' She reached up to kiss his cheek, and there was a hint of a smoulder in his green eyes that sent an answering smoulder through her blood. 'Come in. I'll sort out drinks, and then get the fish fingers going. Tilly, would you like to help me?'

'Yes, please! And I brought my favourite book.'

It was about a black cat rather than a white one, and Jenny smiled. 'We can read it to Sooty together after lunch, if you like.'

She'd already set the table in the dining room; James went to chat with Betty while Jenny tucked a clean tea-towel around Tilly to protect her clothes. Between them, they seasoned the fries with smoked paprika—probably a little more than Jenny would normally have used—and put them in the drawer of the air fryer.

'How high can you count, Tilly?' Jenny asked.

'A hundred,' Tilly said proudly.

It was a while since Jenny had counted with a small child, but she was pretty sure that her brother's children had struggled with the teens at that age, and they'd been bright. 'That many? Wow!'

'Daddy taught me,' Tilly said. 'One, two, skip a few, ninety-nine, one hundred!'

Jenny laughed. 'That's clever! How high do you count at nursery?'

'Twelve. I get a bit muddled after that,' the little girl confessed.

'OK. We need twelve pieces of lettuce, and eight tomatoes,' Jenny said. 'Can you count them out for me?'

Once Tilly had done that and Jenny had washed the vegetables and sliced the tomatoes, they cut the sandwiches together and added the sauces—tomato, of course, for Tilly. When the air fryer beeped, Jenny sent Tilly to call Betty and James to the table.

'I helped,' Tilly said proudly. 'And I counted to a whole hundred.'

Jenny caught James's eye. *Skip a few,* she mouthed, and he grinned back, sharing the joke and enjoying it.

Right then, he looked relaxed and happy, and that grin took her breath away.

Weird how the house felt like a family home again, Jenny thought. Tilly chattering was like the way she and her brother had talked at the dinner table, eager to share what they'd done at school. And Betty was as attentive to Tilly as Jenny's own grandparents had been to her.

Although Betty had burned the apple pie, Jenny tried to avoid serving the worst bits of the crust and covered it with custard. Both James and Tilly declared the pudding delicious; the sheer joy on Betty's face put a lump in Jenny's throat. It was good to see her mother relaxing and unwinding, too. James even got Betty singing snatches of Abba songs and telling stories of the day she'd seen them play in Manchester—something she hadn't talked about in years.

James insisted on doing the washing up, and then Tilly entertained them after lunch, reading her book to Sooty. 'It's all about a greedy cat,' she told Sooty. 'He's a black cat, like you. And, look, that word says "cat",' she said, picking out the word. 'C-a-t,' she spelled, clearly proud that she could read some words.

Although the full text was obviously beyond Tilly's reading ability, she told the story to Sooty with the help of the pictures.

'I've read it to her so often, she knows it almost by heart,' James said very quietly.

And, from the way Tilly was pointing out details in the pictures to Sooty, clearly James had spent time with her rather than rushing it or seeing reading to her as a chore.

Jenny could see from her mother's expression that the little girl had charmed her hugely, too.

Was this what it would've been like, had she had a child with Simon?

Though somehow she couldn't imagine Simon having the same kind of patience with a pre-schooler than James had. He wouldn't have had the same gentleness in his tone when he corrected her on a word.

'Thank you for having me,' Tilly said at the end of the afternoon. 'I've had a lovely time, and so has Daddy.'

And so have we, Jenny thought. James and his daughter had brought a real brightness with them.

'Come and see us any time,' Betty said. 'And I'll dig out my old records, James.'

She'd got rid of the vinyl and the record player years ago, Jenny remembered with a pang. But she'd look on her streaming app and make a special playlist, instead, filling it with the songs her mum could remember.

'I'd like that,' he said with a grin. 'Tell you what, Betty, I think we'd be a good team on a pub music quiz.'

'Let's do it,' Betty said.

'I'll find out when the next one is locally,' James promised.

Jenny saw him to the front door. 'Thank you. Mum's had a lovely afternoon.'

'So have we—haven't we, shrimp?' James asked, sweeping Tilly's mop of curls out of her eyes.

'I'm not a shrimp, I'm a girl.'

'You're a shrimp, and I'm a shark who's going to chase you across the swimming pool this evening,' James teased, and Tilly shrieked with laughter.

'Thank you, Jenny.' He took her hand and squeezed it. 'I enjoyed spending time with you. Maybe we can have dinner sometime this week. Go into Ripon, maybe. Somewhere dressy.'

'Provided you let me pay,' she said.

'We'll argue that later.' He leaned forward and brushed his mouth against hers. 'See you tomorrow,' he said, his voice husky and full of promise.

Jenny stood waving as she watched them go, but mainly because she didn't trust her knees to hold her up after that sweet stolen kiss.

When she went back into the living room, Betty said, 'You've chosen a good one, this time.'

'James is my friend, Mum. My colleague,' Jenny protested.

'He doesn't look at you like a friend,' Betty said. 'I like him. A lot. He's a man with a heart.'

And that was what Jenny was afraid of. Because it would be oh, so easy to let herself fall in love with James Madden and his little girl.

On Monday, James was doing the annual vaccination and health check for a ten-year-old pug called Percy. He noticed that the dog had developed a bit of a pot belly, and his coat was thinning on his flanks.

'Tell me a bit more about Percy, Mr Reynolds,' he said to the owner. 'How's he been, the last six months?'

'I know he's getting a bit fat and his hair's thinning a bit and fading in colours,' Mr Reynolds said, 'but they do say pets look like their owners.' He laughed, patting his own pot belly. 'Seriously, though, he's doing OK. He's maybe eating a bit more than usual, but he's enjoying his walks and he hasn't seemed unwell.'

'Has he been drinking more?'

'And panting a bit, but it's July. Even in England, it can get a bit hot,' Mr Reynolds said.

Which sounded to James as if Mr Reynolds was trying very hard not to notice any changes, worrying that it might be something serious and not being able to face it. 'Have you noticed anything different in the way he's behaved?'

Mr Reynolds thought for a moment. 'I guess he's started wanting to go out for a wee in the middle of the night—but he's ten. Isn't that normal?'

'Not really,' James said.

Mr Reynolds looked anxious. 'Is there something wrong with him, do you think?'

'I think he might have developed a medical condition,' James said, 'but, if it's what I think it is, it's something we can give him medication for and he'll do just fine.'

'Me and Percy, we've been together ten years. He saw me through when I lost my wife,' Mr Reynolds said. 'Without him…' He swallowed hard. 'What's wrong with him?'

'I'd like to do a blood test to check, but I think he might have a bit of a problem with his hormones.'

'He's not going to die?'

James knew he had to phrase this carefully. 'Most dogs with this condition are absolutely fine with medication,' he said. 'May I do a blood test?'

Mr Reynolds' eyes widened as he took in

the possible severity, and he rubbed the top of the pug's head. 'Yes, of course. Whatever you need. And I'll do whatever it takes to make him well. I know I let him have too many treats, and if it's my fault that he's fat...'

'No, it's not your fault,' James said, seeing the anxiety in Mr Reynolds' expression. 'But I agree, it's a good idea to scale the treats back a little bit. Dogs are like humans; as they get older, they don't need quite so many calories.'

He deftly took a blood sample, and then made a fuss of the dog. 'I might need to do a second test, depending on the results of this one. Would you be able to sit in the waiting room for a while, Mr Reynolds, or would you rather come back tomorrow?'

'I'll wait,' Mr Reynolds said. 'I want my boy made better.'

'Thank you,' James said.

He ushered Mr Reynolds and Percy out of the consulting room, then went into the back room where Anu, their veterinary nurse, was assessing the animals who'd come in for a procedure.

'Are you rushed off your feet, Anu, or can you run a couple of blood tests for me, please?' he asked.

'I can run the tests. What do you need?'

'Baseline,' he said, 'and I want to take a close look at liver enzymes, thyroid and cortisol levels.'

'Hormone tests?' Jenny asked, coming into the room and clearly overhearing the last bit.

'I suspect we have a dog with Cushing's,' James said. 'Depending on what the blood results are, I'm planning to do a low-dose dexamethasone suppression test.'

'Which dog?' Jenny asked.

'Percy.'

'Mr Reynolds' pug,' she said. 'I noticed at Percy's last check-up that he'd put on some weight. I was thinking possible thyroid, given Percy's hair was thinning and losing colour, but Cushing's makes sense. Let me know how he gets on. Mr Reynolds lives on the same road as Mum and me, and I see him pass our house every morning on his walk. He always waves to Mum, or stops and has a chat if she's out in the garden. If I can do anything to support him, I will.'

'Will do,' James said.

His next patient was a kitten in for vaccinations and microchipping; by the time they'd finished discussing worming and neutering, the blood tests were done.

'High liver enzymes, low thyroid, and too much cortisol,' James said.

'You're right. That definitely sounds like hyperadrenocorticism,' Jenny said.

He nodded. 'I'm planning a low-dose dexamethasone suppression test.' It meant giving the pug an injection of steroid and taking blood samples over the next eight hours to measure Percy's cortisol levels; dogs with Cushing's found it harder to lower their cortisol levels after an injection.

'If there's a tumour...just to warn you... Mr Reynolds lost his wife to cancer five years ago,' Jenny told him quietly.

'He did say he'd lost his wife, but it felt rude to ask how. Thank you—I'll make sure I'm careful how I phrase it,' James said.

She patted his arm. 'I know you'll be careful. I just thought you could do with a headsup, in the circumstances.'

James called Mr Reynolds and Percy back into the consulting room, and made a fuss of Percy. 'He's a lovely little fellow.'

'My best boy. Mary and I couldn't have children,' Mr Reynolds said. 'What did the blood test say? Is he going to be all right?'

Remembering what Jenny had told him, James faced Mr Reynolds and smiled in reassurance. 'I think he has a condition called Cushing's disease—it's where the body produces too much cortisol. The good news is that we can give him medication to control the symptoms, so you should find his fur's in better condition, he doesn't drink so much or need to go out in the middle of the night, and he'll lose that little pot belly.'

Mr Reynolds' shoulders sagged. 'Thank God. I thought you were going to tell me...' His voice broke.

'He should be with you for a few years yet,' James reassured him. He drew a quick sketch. 'Now, I've checked Percy's records, so I know he hasn't suffered any allergies or an immune disorder that needed to be treated with steroids, which is a possible cause of Cushing's.'

'So what's causing it?' Mr Reynolds asked.

'It's a hormone imbalance. The pituitary gland is here, at the base of the brain—' James marked it on his sketch '—and it sends a message to the adrenal gland to produce cortisol.' He marked the adrenal gland next to the kidney, and chose his next words very carefully. 'Sometimes there's a benign growth on the adrenal gland or on the pituitary gland, which affects the way the hormones are produced and causes the kind of symptoms Percy's been getting.'

Mr Reynolds paled. 'Percy's got cancer?'

'No,' James said. 'It's usually a benign growth.' And he really, really hoped that this wasn't one of the rare malignant cases.

'Will he need an operation? I mean, he's not a young dog, any more. If he...' Mr Reynolds dragged in a breath. 'I'm sorry I'm making such a fuss.'

'Don't be. You and Percy are family, and it's always a shock to hear when our dogs aren't well,' James reassured him. 'In most cases, there's a growth—and again, I'd like to emphasise they tend to be benign—on the pituitary gland, but sometimes it's on the adrenal gland. I need to see which gland is affected, so I can give Percy the right treatment. The good news is that the treatment's a capsule, and you can disguise it in a treat.'

'Don't you need to send him for a scan?'

James shook his head. 'I could, but apart from the fact scans are expensive it also means he'll need to be sedated to keep him still while he's being scanned. As you said, he's not a young dog, so I'd rather not put him through that if we don't have to. I can find out what I need to know by giving Percy an injection of steroids, then doing a couple more blood tests over the rest of the day. It'll be a lot easier on his system.'

'All right,' Mr Reynolds said. 'Can I wait with him?'

'I know it's hard,' James said gently, 'but it'll be easier if you go home, Mr Reynolds. Percy can settle here and rest without worrying about you. And I promise I'll call you the minute I've got the results, and then he can come home.'

Mr Reynolds bit his lip, then made a last fuss of Percy. 'Be a good boy for Dr Madden, here.'

'He'll be fine,' James said. 'And he'll get to have a fuss made of him by every single person in the practice. We all love dogs and we all want to see Percy his usual well and happy self.'

Mr Reynolds nodded, took a deep breath—clearly he was close to tears—and handed Percy's lead to James. 'I trust you with my boy.'

'We'll take good care of him,' James said.

Once Mr Reynolds had gone, James gave Percy an injection of steroids and found him a comfortable spot in the kennels area. He did the first blood sample an hour later, between seeing patients in morning surgery, then caught up with paperwork over a sandwich at his desk before beginning the afternoon surgery.

With it being summer, it was prime tick season; he had a couple of dogs in with swollen armpits, and taught the owners how to spot ticks and remove them safely with a tick-twisting tool before advising them to add tick and flea treatment to their worming routine. 'It doesn't stop the ticks biting, but if they're infected it kills them before they can spread Lyme disease,' he explained.

One of the dogs had reacted particularly badly to the tick bite, so he prescribed antibiotics. 'Keep an eye on him. If he's still off his food in a week, or if you notice any sign of swollen joints, lethargy or a fever, bring him straight back,' he said. 'I'll have a note on his file, so even if we're busy we'll make sure we see him.'

Jenny was checking a cat who'd needed some teeth out in the back room when James checked his last sample.

'Is that Percy's blood test?' she asked.

'Yes. It's definitely Cushing's, and it's the pituitary involved,' James said.

'So you can treat him with daily capsules

rather than putting him through surgery. Good,' she said. 'I meant to ask—is there any news on your house, yet?'

'Moving day's confirmed for a week on Saturday,' he said. 'Which gives me another two weeks to get the house sorted out ready for Tilly's birthday party. Sophie organised the pre-schooler party for me last year, and I'm ashamed to say I haven't a clue where to start. I've spent the last three nights looking things up on the internet.' He wrinkled his nose. 'So far, I've got a list of party games, and I know I need to make sure that every-one wins a prize or a sticker in every single game, with a slightly bigger prize for the win-ner. And that needs to be a different person each game, too.'

'That sounds pretty good to me,' she said. 'What are you doing for a birthday cake?'

'Cake-making isn't in my skill set. Luckily, Mum's coming to the rescue. She's borrow-ing a cake tin in the shape of a number four.'

'Good idea,' she said. 'What's the theme?'

'Theme?' He looked blankly at her. 'Is "pink" a theme?'

'I guess,' she said. 'Or fairies, or unicorns.'

'I did think puppies,' he said. 'But Sir Woofalot isn't coming home until after her party. I thought ten excited four-year-olds might be a bit too much for a pup.'

'Definitely,' she agreed. 'You're having Reuben's pup, then?'

'I asked Ben if he'd mind us having a pup, and he said it was fine. So, yes,' he said. 'Reuben's happy—oh, and his calves are all doing well. The first lot will be out of quarantine in a day or two, and the second lot had a much easier time of it because we caught them early.'

'That's good. It sounds as if everything's coming together for you. That's lovely.'

'Thanks.' And everything in his new life was going to plan. A job he loved with colleagues he really liked, his daughter had settled at nursery and made friends that would help her settle in to school, and they were about to move into their own place and get a pup.

The only thing missing was someone to share it with.

Though Jenny was helping him with that, overcoming his rusty social skills.

'Is Tamsin able to sit with your mum on Thursday night?' he asked.

She nodded. 'Did you want to run birthday stuff past me over dinner?'

'I was thinking more the other project,' he said.

Just for a second, she looked flustered. And then she smiled. 'Sure.' She glanced at her watch. 'You'd better call Mr Reynolds.'

'And Percy will be thrilled to see him,' James agreed. He called Mr Reynolds to tell him Percy was ready to be picked up. When Mr Reynolds came in, his eyes were rimmed with red, as if he'd been crying with relief.

'The good news is, we can treat Percy with a capsule once a day to reduce the production of cortisol, and it will help his symptoms,' James said. 'You need to give him the capsule whole, with a meal, so I'd suggest disguising it in a treat before you give him his dinner.'

'I will,' Mr Reynolds said.

'You might find the hair loss gets a little bit worse before it improves,' James warned, 'but you should start to see a difference in a couple of weeks. I've printed off a leaflet for you that explains everything, but ring me if you're the slightest bit worried.'

'What if I forget to give him a dose?' Mr Reynolds asked.

'Then you just wait to give him his normal

dose, the next day—don't give him double,' James said. 'Most dogs tolerate the treatment just fine, but if Percy's sick or has diarrhoea, bring him straight back to us. I'd like to see him once a week for the next three weeks, to see how he gets on, and then we can go a bit longer in between visits. But I promise we'll keep a good eye on him, Mr Reynolds.'

'Thank you,' Mr Reynolds said, shaking his hand.

It was good to be able to help with someone's worries and bring a bit of sunshine into their life, James thought. Which was what Jenny was doing for him. And maybe he could find a way to do that for her, too.

CHAPTER SIX

DINNER.

This wasn't just a meal with a friend, where it didn't matter what she wore. It was a practice date. One that made Jenny realise just how rusty she was when it came to dating. Thankfully her favourite little black dress still fitted, and it was a classic style that wouldn't look dated. She made an effort to style her hair into soft waves, instead of pulling it back into a scrunchie, the way she normally wore it, and dredged out a pair of high heels. A touch of lipstick and mascara, and she was ready.

'You look lovely,' Betty said. 'Are you going out with James?'

'We're just friends, Mum,' Jenny said. Explaining the situation would be too complicated, and her mum would worry. 'We're simply having a nice time together, as colleagues, relaxing after work.'

'Hmm. Is Archer going as well?' Betty said.

'He can't make it tonight,' Jenny fibbed, feeling guilty that they hadn't asked Archer.

'Well, I like James.'

'So do I. As a *friend*,' Jenny emphasised. Secretly, she was beginning to suspect that she liked him as a little bit more than a friend, but she didn't have the headspace to work it out.

Tamsin came over with a playlist on her phone, some home-made cheese shortbread and a bottle of a non-alcoholic cocktail to share with Betty; then, at precisely seven, the doorbell rang.

James was wearing a dark blue suit with a white shirt and copper-coloured tie, and he didn't look like the slightly scruffy but professional colleague she was used to.

'You look lovely,' he said.

'Thank you—so do you,' she said, feeling oddly shy.

After he'd exchanged a few words with Betty and Tamsin, James drove Jenny to the foodie pub, two villages away, where he'd booked a table.

'I can't remember the last time I went out to dinner like this,' he said. 'I'm more used to places that do the kind of food Tilly likes.'

And Jenny wasn't used to going out to dinner at all, any more. She glanced down the menu and chuckled. 'You can bring her here, you know—they offer cod goujons.'

'Ah, but they're *posh* fish fingers,' he said, laughing back.

'The menu's fabulous. It's really hard to choose,' she said. In the end, she chose salmon served with Tenderstem broccoli, asparagus, courgettes and new potatoes, while James plumped for pie and mash with greens.

'That's so blokey,' she said with a grin.

'It's a treat,' he corrected. 'Because I'd never cook pie and mash for myself.'

'I was under the impression,' she said, 'that you cooked.'

'I can shove something on a tray in the oven and forget about it for thirty minutes,' he said, 'and I think anyone can manage vegetables with an electric steamer. But that doesn't really count as cooking, does it?'

'Not really,' she agreed.

'Mum taught me a few basics before I went to university,' he said, 'but I was never really interested in cooking. Some of my friends could woo their girlfriends with home-made lasagne, but mine would get cheese on toast if they were lucky. Or pasta mixed with pesto.'

'Maybe we should put the practice dating on hold and do some cookery lessons instead, once you've moved into the cottage,' she said. 'Tilly can join in.'

'A small child and a sharp knife?' He looked horrified.

'A small child, a wooden spoon and a mixing bowl,' she corrected.

'If you're really offering, then, yes, please,' he said. 'Just don't let on to my mum quite how hopeless I am.'

'It'll be our secret. And Tilly's and Mum's,' she added.

'What you were saying about putting the practice dating on hold.' James looked at her. 'You're struggling as hard as I am with this situation, aren't you?'

'It's just...odd,' she admitted. 'At work, you and I talk about our patients. In Burndale, we have Tilly and my mum with us. But here...' It *felt* like a real date, despite their protests that it wasn't. And that made her insides feel as if they'd done an anatomically impossible backflip.

'If it makes you feel better,' James said, 'I'm relieved that you're finding it difficult. That means I'm not alone.'

Which meant that she wasn't alone, either.

But the conversation stalled again, and they just looked at each other.

In the end, James laughed. 'You know what?' He picked up his phone. 'I know it's rude to check my phone when we're out, but we're both very obviously stuck on this. Let's ask the internet what you do on a first date.'

They'd agreed on the way to the pub to keep their phones on the table, face down, in case of emergencies—even though they knew Tilly would be perfectly fine with James's mum and her own mother would be fine with Tamsin, they both wanted the comfort of knowing that they were only a phone call away if there was a problem.

'Questions to ask your first date. Are you an early bird or a night owl?' James read. 'Oh, wait—this is a good one. Are you a cat person or a dog person?'

Jenny laughed. 'As vets, we're both—and both.'

'Hobbies—right, we both have time for them. Not.' He rolled his eyes.

'Actually, that's a good one. Archer makes time for his sky-watching. What would you do, if you had the time?' she asked.

'Visit every single castle in Yorkshire, and

make sure I get the best view from the highest point,' he said. 'You?'

'Actually, that's not so far off what I do at weekends,' she said. 'Mum and I tend to visit the gardens rather than the stately homes or ruined castles—unless they've got good accessibility.'

'And ruins, by definition, don't,' he said. 'But we could make it work. Take it in turns to explore the inaccessible bits while the other one eats ice cream in the tea shop with Tilly and your mum.'

'Let's add that to our list,' she said. 'What else?'

'To add to our list?' he asked.

She shook her head. 'We're not discussing the safe stuff. What else would you do, if you had the time?'

'Travel,' he said. 'Anna and I used to love city breaks. We'd do maybe one or two of the top ten tourist attractions in the city, but then we'd wander off in the back streets and see what we could find.'

'Living in the city, Simon and I always headed for the countryside rather than the city,' Jenny said. 'I think my favourite break was in Iceland. We got to see a geyser, loads of waterfalls—that was fabulous, because there were rainbows everywhere, and the best one we actually got to stand behind the waterfall and look out. And there's this amazing beach that had hexagonal columns of basalt. I loved that—the contrast between the turquoise sea and the black sandy beach.'

'It sounds great,' he said. 'I've always wanted to do the coast-to-coast walk from Whitehaven to Whitby. But I couldn't possibly expect Tilly's little legs to keep up on something like that.'

'We could do bits of the walk, in the Dales,' she said.

He smiled. 'We could—but if we start planning things like that, making a list of the parts that'd be accessible for your mum and Tilly, it takes us out of dating territory.' He glanced at his phone. 'Back to the list of questions. Is Iceland your favourite travel memory?'

'Yes, because the landscape's so different,' she said. 'I loved the waterfalls, and then the little hot pot spa pools—there seemed to be one in every town.'

'Did you see the Northern Lights?' he asked.

'We went in summer, so we saw the midnight sun instead,' she said. 'It was a real experience, walking by the harbour in Reykjavik at midnight and watching the sun just about setting over the sea.'

'I'd like to see that, one day,' he said. 'And the Northern Lights. If we could all have time off together, I'm pretty sure Archer would be up for a Burnham Veterinary Surgery bonding trip to see the Northern Lights.'

'He would,' Jenny agreed. 'They're on my bucket list, too. But they've been seen in Yorkshire. I'm pretty sure Archer gets text alerts or something about potential aurora nights.'

'Maybe we can have a team Northern Lights-spotting outing, with him in charge, next time he gets an alert,' James said with a smile.

'What's your favourite travel memory?' Jenny asked.

'Venice,' he said immediately. 'Dancing in St Mark's Square on a late spring evening when hardly anyone was about. We put one earphone in each and played something soppy on my phone.'

'Simon wasn't really one for dancing,' Jenny said, feeling a twinge of envy.

The relationship she'd had with Simon sounded like a shadow of what James and Anna had had. And she could really see James's problem. He clearly loved Anna so deeply that, despite him saying he wanted and needed to move on, she wasn't sure he'd be able to. How would any woman be able to measure up to memories like those?

'If you like dancing,' he said, 'we can find somewhere to dance.'

The idea of having a slow dance with James, under the lights of the stars and the moon, made a shiver of anticipation run down her spine. What would it feel like to be in his arms? Cradled close, swaying together to a slow beat…

But it wasn't going to happen, and she couldn't afford to let herself dream about it. 'I'm not really one for clubbing. What's the next question on your list?' she asked.

'What matters to you?' he asked. 'But I know that. Your mum and your job. Just as you know my answer.'

'Tilly and your job,' she said. 'Next?'

He scanned the list. 'An awful lot of them are things we already know about each other. This isn't helping.' He flicked to another page. 'Oh, and here are topics not to talk about. Wait for it: family, parents and exes.' He groaned. 'Oh, dear.'

She laughed. 'We've done just about all of those.'

'According to this, we should keep conversation light and unpressured. Casual chit-chat.'

'Which would bore you silly,' Jenny said.

'And you,' James said.

'What's your idea of the perfect romantic day?' she asked after their food had arrived.

'It'd be spring,' he said. 'Breakfast on the coast, somewhere we can see the sunrise—preferably with a bacon sandwich, and a mug of tea you can stand your spoon up in. Then a walk on the beach, to see if we can find fossils. Heading out through the Dales, along one of the back roads where you see lambs skipping about in the fields and new calves all wobbly on their legs. Lunch in a little old pub somewhere—and, because we'd be walking it off, that'd involve Yorkshire pudding, locally produced sausages and cauliflower cheese. A walk round a ruined castle, watching the sun set somewhere, and then dinner somewhere like this followed by dancing under the stars.'

It sounded like her idea of the perfect romantic day, too. Which was really unsettling, because now she could imagine sharing something like that with James, and it made butterflies rampage in her tummy.

'You?' he asked.

She thought about making up something exotic, but he already knew her so well that he'd spot at once that it was a fib. 'That'd work for me, too,' she said. 'Though I'll switch that tea for good coffee, and there had better be scones with cream and jam in the afternoon. Actually, I think I'd start in the Dales, going via a waterfall or two, and head towards the coast. Then the dancing after dinner could be barefoot on the beach, seeing the moon make a path on the sea.'

'That,' he said, 'sounds even better than my version.'

The possibility hung in the air between them.

A romantic day. Just the two of them. Nothing to worry about other than holding hands, having fun, dancing under the stars and kissing in the moonlight.

Jenny was shocked to realise that she was actually leaning slightly towards him, as if they were already together on that date. Which was crazy, because no way did either of their lives have room for a day like that. 'It's fun to dream,' she said instead, trying to get the lightness back between them instead of the sudden tension. 'And now you've got your benchmark for your dates. On the first day, you ask her about her idea of a perfect romantic date. If it doesn't match yours, then maybe you're not suited.'

Though she didn't dare meet his eyes, in case he could see what she had a nasty feeling might be written in hers.

The following weekend, James spent Saturday moving into the cottage. He'd put most of his personal things plus his furniture into storage; he'd hired a removals company to bring it to the cottage, and Archer, his parents and his sister were helping him to move and unpack.

Jenny had suggested that Tilly could spend moving day with her and Betty, so James wouldn't have to worry about his daughter while he was getting the house straight.

'I can't ask you to do that. That's above and beyond friendship,' he said.

'It's what friends do for each other,' she contradicted. 'Anyway, you're not asking me. I'm offering. And I'd really like you to say yes, because Mum's looking forward to fish fingers for lunch, and doing a bit of singing with Tilly and playing games with her.'

He gave in gratefully. 'Thank you,' he said. 'It's really appreciated.'

The cottage was typical for the area: stone, with a slate roof and a front garden bursting with old-fashioned cottage garden flowers that scented the air. There were three good-sized bedrooms: one for himself, one for Tilly and one for guests. He took Tilly to the house first, to show her where they were going to live, and let her choose which bedroom she wanted before dropping her off at Jenny's. Predictably, she chose the one with pink curtains that overlooked the garden and was next to his.

His parents, his sister and Archer arrived and helped him move all the furniture and boxes, as well as putting Tilly's new princess bed together with its filmy pale pink drapes.

'She'll be thrilled to bits when she sees that,' his mum said with a smile.

James had bought a new bed for himself, too, wanting a new start. He'd given the bed he'd shared with Anna to a women's refuge, knowing his wife would've approved thoroughly of his decision.

They worked solidly throughout the day, only stopping briefly for the bacon rolls and Yorkshire parkin James had ordered from

Sally at the café—and which Sally had insisted on delivering herself.

'You OK?' James's mum asked.

He nodded. 'It's just a bit...strange. It's home, but not home at the same time.'

She gave him a hug. 'I know you loved Anna, but she'd be the first person to tell you to move on. And Jenny's lovely. She was so kind to me when we had to say goodbye to Treacle. She gave me all the time I needed to be with him on that last morning, let me weep all over her and even made me a cup of tea.' She paused. 'Anna would've liked her very much.'

There was a lump in his throat. James agreed. Anna would've liked Jenny.

But.

'Jenny's my friend.'

'I know, love, but all I want is for you to be happy. I'm just trying to say, I can't see any barriers to making your friendship something more.' She hugged him again. 'Our Tilly's taken a real shine to her.'

Which was a relief, but he knew it wasn't a given that Jenny would want to make a family with them. 'We're friends,' James insisted.

But when he'd gone out to dinner with Jenny and talked about their perfect romantic day, they'd been really in tune. They'd wanted the same things. She'd even told him to use it as a benchmark when he started dating. Did that mean she'd use their shared idea of a perfect romantic day as a benchmark, too? Would she consider dating him for real, despite the fact that he came as a package?

Though Jenny had her own complications to deal with. James wasn't entirely sure whether she was still quietly in love with her ex and using her mum's illness as an excuse not to date anyone. The last thing he wanted was to scare her off.

'Speaking of Jenny, she's had Tilly all day. I'd better call her and let her know I can pick Tilly up,' he said, and took his phone out of his pocket.

Jenny answered quickly. 'Hi, James. How's the moving?'

'All done,' he said. 'I can come and collect Tilly now.'

'I have a better idea,' she said. 'Why don't I bring Tilly and Mum, and stop at the fish and chip shop on the way? I can pick up an order for everyone,' she said, 'and we can celebrate your new house. And we can eat from the wrappers, so you're not left with a pile of washing up.'

She really did think of everything. 'That would be wonderful,' James said. 'Thank you. But only on condition that you tell me how much it is, so I can transfer the money to you. I really think I should be the one treating everyone.'

'We'll sort it out later,' Jenny said. 'Go and ask everyone what they want, and text me the order. See you in a bit.'

James checked with his family and Archer, and texted the order to Jenny.

A few minutes later, Jenny arrived with her mum, Tilly and the food.

'I had a really nice day, Daddy,' Tilly said. 'I drawed you a picture of Sooty, and me and Betty read to Sooty, and we did singing, and we made fairy cakes with sprinkles.'

'Otherwise known as pudding—we brought them over,' Jenny said with a smile, and handed him a carrier bag containing two bottles of Prosecco and two bottles of sparkling elderflower cordial. 'Plus some bubbles to celebrate your new house, including the non-alcoholic version.'

'You,' James said, meaning it, 'are a marvel.'

She shrugged it off, but he could see the sparkle in her eyes and the heightened colour in her cheeks.

'I stirred everything,' Tilly said when everyone had finished their fish and chips and Jenny had brought out the tin of cakes, 'and I put it in the cake cases, and Jenny put it in the oven. And then I stirred the icing and put it on top with the sprinkles. Lots and lots and lots of sprinkles.'

'They're perfect,' James's mother said, giving her a kiss.

'Do you want to come and see your room, Tilly?' James asked.

Tilly nodded with excitement and clutched Jenny's hand. 'Jenny, will you come and see my room, too?'

Jenny was touched that the little girl wanted her to see the room; but, at the same time, maybe this particular moment should be for just James. She glanced at him for guidance, and he smiled at her. 'Come and have a look round,' he said.

'You've all done wonders. I was expecting to see lots of boxes, still,' she said.

He laughed. 'I've barely touched my books, but Tilly's room is done.'

'Daddy! You made me a real princess bed! A pink one!' Tilly squealed in delight as she opened the door. 'I love it!'

There were fairy lights twirling round the columns at the corners of the bed, too, and round the fireplace.

'And you put Mummy's picture up,' she said, looking happy.

Of course Jenny couldn't resist glancing at the framed photograph on the mantelpiece over the fireplace.

Anna was stunningly beautiful, with the same long dark curls and huge brown eyes as Tilly, and it looked as if Tilly had inherited her mother's bone structure, too. But it wasn't just that Anna was beautiful on the outside: her personality shone through the photograph, the kind of smile that told you she was the sort who loved life and made everyone else's life just that bit brighter for being in it.

How much both James and Tilly had lost.

Jenny's heart ached for them. 'Your mummy looks lovely,' she said. 'She's got a beautiful smile. And she's so like you.'

Tilly looked pleased. 'My other nanna says I'm her spitting image. And my nanna here says I'm as sweet as my mummy was.' She smiled. 'You're lovely, too, Jenny. You're all smiley and nice.'

'Thank you, sweetheart.' Jenny didn't dare look at James. It would be just too awkward. She wasn't in competition with Anna and she didn't want him to feel that she was trying to take Anna's place. 'You have a pretty view over the garden.'

The little girl nodded. 'That's where Sir Woofalot and me are going to play, when I get my puppy. One day,' she added wistfully.

This time, Jenny did look at James; behind Tilly's back, he winked at her and put his finger to his lips in a 'shh' signal. Clearly the puppy was going to stay a secret for now—as was her grandmother's new pup.

'We'd better go down and join the others,' Jenny said. 'Your room's lovely, Tilly.'

When they went back downstairs, Jenny could see that her mum was getting tired. 'We need to get back,' she said with a smile. 'Catch you on Monday at work, James. Bye, Tilly!' She took her leave of the rest of James's family and Archer, and drove Betty home.

She still wasn't sure if James was really ready to move on.

And, if he was—would it be with her? Or would he be better off with someone who had fewer complications?

CHAPTER SEVEN

PERCY THE PUG came in for a check-up, the following week. 'He's doing really well,' James reassured Mr Reynolds, his owner. 'He'll be on the daily treatment for the rest of his life, and we'll do regular checks and blood tests to keep an eye on him.'

'He's definitely more his old self—not panting so much, and not hungry all the time. That little pot belly's starting to go,' Mr Reynolds said.

'I'm really glad,' James said.

He caught up with Jenny at lunchtime. 'Good news—Percy the pug came in for a check-up and he's responding to his meds. I'm happy with the blood test I did today.'

'Oh, that's fabulous,' Jenny said. 'I bet Mr Reynolds is relieved.'

'I'm glad I've caught you both,' Archer said, walking into the staff room. 'Just letting you know that we have a vacancy for a part-time vet nurse—Anu handed her notice in yesterday morning. She wants to move to Hull with her boyfriend.'

'I had a feeling that might be on the cards,' Jenny said. 'We'll miss her—she's so good with the owners as well as their pets.'

'She wants to go earlier rather than stay to work out her notice,' Archer said.

'Can you get hold of a locum so she can go?' James asked.

'Better than that,' Archer said. 'I've got someone locally who's happy to step in for a little while.' His ears went very pink again. 'Halley. She…um…it'll be just for a few months.'

'And will she stay on when her maternity leave ends?' Jenny asked very gently.

He sighed. 'The whole village is talking about it, aren't they?'

'About the fact that she's pregnant and you're moving in together?' James asked. 'I've heard a mention or two. But it's not gossip, Arch. Everyone's really thrilled for you both.' He clapped a hand on Archer's shoulder. 'I remember you liked her years ago, when we were at school. I couldn't be happier for you.' He left it unspoken, but was pretty sure that his best friend would be able to read it in his eyes: after all the sadness he'd been through with Amy, Archer deserved a break.

Archer looked at them. 'As we've brought up village gossip, I'm not the only one they're talking about. Is there anything you want to tell me?'

'I need a mum for Tilly. I haven't dated for ten years—so I need a female friend to bring me up to speed on the dating front, which is where Jenny comes in,' James said, not looking at Jenny.

'And, with Mum to look after, I just don't have the headspace for a proper relationship right now,' Jenny said. 'So being James's dating coach works for me. It means I get to have some fun without the pressure, and Mum stops worrying that she's wrecked my social life—which of course she hasn't, but she's worried anyway.'

This time, James did look at Jenny, and was relieved to see her smiling. 'Though it's a shame we're being talked about. I thought we'd managed to avoid people seeing us together.'

'By going for a drink in a pub that's only a couple of villages away? I think you'd have to go to the other side of the North York Moors before you'd be off the Burndale gossip radar,' Archer said ruefully.

'Jenny and I are just good friends—and colleagues,' James said.

'Absolutely,' Jenny agreed.

'Hmm.' Archer didn't look entirely convinced. 'Well, anyway, I just wanted to let you know about Halley joining us.'

'Was he trying to deflect what's going on between him and Halley, or are people *really* talking about us?' James asked when Archer had left.

'They're probably gossiping,' Jenny said. 'But you know what it's like in a small village. Blink and they'll be talking about something else. How are the plans coming on for Tilly's birthday?'

'We've invited all the girls she's friends with at nursery, so if they all come there will be about ten of them, including Tilly,' he said. 'I've come up with a menu Mum agrees with—cream cheese sandwiches cut into stars, cocktail sausages, cherry tomatoes, carrot sticks, pitta chips and hummus, and then we're doing a "build your own sundae" with ice cream, strawberry slices, squirty cream in a can, sprinkles and a chocolate flake.'

'That sounds messy, but fun,' she said. 'What about a birthday cake?'

'Mum's making the cake for me and icing it.' He grinned. 'Guess what colour it's going to be?'

'Let me think—oh—could it possibly be a shade of flamingo, cerise or carnation?' she asked, laughing back.

'Certainly is,' he said. 'I need to put together some goodie bags. Going by what Tilly likes, I was thinking bubbles, coloured pencils and a colouring book, some playdough and a cutter, and maybe a pack of flower seeds. And I can pack them in pink paper carrier bags.'

'Sounds good,' she said. 'You've really got this sorted.'

'Once I stopped panicking and made a few lists, it got a bit easier,' he admitted.

'Good.' She smiled at him.

'Are you busy Thursday evening?' he asked. 'For…um…project planning? I thought we could go to Aysgarth and have a walk, then a picnic by the falls.'

'That'd be lovely,' she agreed.

Thursday evening was perfect weather for a walk, warm enough not to need a jacket but not humid. James's mum was babysitting

Tilly and Jenny's neighbour Sheila was keeping Betty company. Jenny had put together a picnic, and he drove them out to Aysgarth.

The falls were a popular tourist spot, but it tended to be busier in the daytime and quieter in the evening, so they had no trouble parking. James thoroughly enjoyed wandering along the bank of the River Ure with Jenny until they reached the broad limestone steps of the waterfall.

Although he hadn't intended to hold her hand, his fingers brushed against hers several times and it felt natural to link his fingers through hers. She didn't pull away, and James told himself that this was just how it would be on a date with a stranger...except somehow he rather doubted it, because he couldn't imagine holding hands with anyone else. It was *Jenny's* hand he wanted to hold.

But he also didn't want to scare her away, so he didn't draw attention to the fact that they were holding hands.

They kept the conversation light, and he took several photographs of the two of them with the waterfalls in the background, as well as some of the round holes in the rock made by spinning water over the years, and a video of the water gushing over the limestone.

'Tilly would love this. We need to do this again in the spring,' Jenny said. 'Even better if we do it a day or so after there's been a lot of rain, so we get to see the waterfalls in full spate. And spring means the primroses and bluebells will be out.'

If she wanted to make plans for months in the future, that was fine by him. 'Great idea,' he said.

He enjoyed the picnic, too, once he'd helped Jenny spread the picnic rug on the ground and unpack the basket. She'd packed fresh bread, a large chunk of crumbly Wensleydale, sweet plum tomatoes and home-made sausage rolls spiced with chili jam, followed by raspberries and Greek yogurt and some sticky Yorkshire parkin he guessed she'd made herself.

'This was perfect,' he said, when she'd packed everything away in the picnic basket.

'Thank you.' She smiled at him.

He took a risk. 'Or almost perfect. There's one more thing that would make this perfect.'

Her blue eyes went wide. 'What?'

'Dance with me? I'm a bit out of practice, but I'll try not to bruise your toes.' He stood up and held his hand out to her. When she took his hand, he drew her to her feet, then took a wireless earbud from his pocket and handed it to her. Once she'd put it into her ear and he'd switched on his own earbud, he started playing the music he'd prepared earlier in the week.

'Just so you know,' he said quietly, 'this isn't what I danced to in Venice with Anna. This one's a song that makes me think of you.'

As soon as Jenny heard the opening notes, she recognised One Direction's 'What Makes You Beautiful'.

This song made him think of her? A song about someone who didn't know how beautiful she was?

The idea made her catch her breath. He'd just strayed well over the lines of 'practice date' territory. She ought to take a step backwards, make some kind of excuse and not dance with him.

But, for the life of her, she couldn't resist the temptation to be in his arms.

She moved closer, resting her head on his shoulder and swaying with him to the beat of the music. It was just the two of them, dancing on the grass by the river, with the rush of the river acting as a backbeat for the music playing in one ear.

He followed up the song with a ballad from

Take That, Eva Cassidy's version of 'Fields of Gold', and Norah Jones—the sweetest, most romantic music she knew. He'd really put some thought and effort into this, and she appreciated it.

When he shifted slightly so his cheek was next to hers, how could she resist kissing the corner of his mouth? And, when he moved a little closer and kissed the corner of her mouth, how could she not respond and move a little closer, until they were really kissing?

The way he kissed her drove every coherent thought out of her head. With her eyes closed, all she was aware of was the warmth of his arms around her, the way his heart thudded against her and the sweetness of his mouth moving against hers.

When James finally broke the kiss, there was a huge slash of colour across his cheeks, and his pupils were so huge that his green eyes looked almost black.

'Sorry,' he said. 'I know I've crossed a line.'

'You have. But I was with you all the way,' she admitted.

'So what do we do now?' he asked.

'I don't know.' She dragged in a breath. 'With Mum's health, I just don't have the space in my life for anything more than friendship.'

'I understand.' He stroked her cheek. 'If I'm completely honest, I don't really have space in my life, either. Not with Tilly. But, if I did, I'd want to share that space with you.'

'Same for me,' she admitted. 'I know you're looking for a mum for Tilly, and I don't want to get in the way.'

'Maybe,' he said, 'we can just avoid making a decision for now.'

'Leaving us both in limbo?' That would be the worst of all worlds, not knowing where they stood or what either of them wanted.

'No. I mean giving us both space to decide what we want,' he said. 'I know I said I want a mum for Tilly, but I don't have to rush into finding a partner. Neither do you.'

'So, what? We stick to being just good friends?'

'Or maybe,' he said, 'we just take the pressure off and see what happens. See where this thing between us goes. I like you, Jenny, and I think you like me.'

She did.

Very much.

But, if it went wrong, the way she'd got it wrong before with Simon, this time there would be collateral damage, and that wasn't fair. Tilly and Betty didn't deserve to be hurt. 'We can't be selfish about this.'

'I know. But let's not overthink things. Maybe there's a way to get what's best for all of us. I know you're a planner, but we don't need to work it out right this very second.' He leaned forward and kissed the tip of her nose, and the cherishing gesture nearly undid her.

'Right now, we both need to be getting back,' he said. 'Even though I'd like to dance with you properly in the moonlight.'

'Next to a waterfall's probably not the best place to do that,' she said, her voice slightly shaky. 'If we trip over a root or an awkward bit of stone…'

'We'll end up falling in. You're right,' he said. 'We need a flat, sandy beach or a lawn.'

She could imagine dancing with him under the light of the moon, to the sound of the waves swooshing onto the shore or the sweet harmony of a nightingale or a robin singing in the garden, and it made her weak at the knees.

He folded the rug, tucked it into the top of the picnic basket, and carried it in one hand while he slid his other arm round Jenny's waist.

'James,' she asked, 'is this a good idea?'

'Yes,' he said. 'I've just kissed you until my common sense went over the edge with the waterfall. *And*,' he added, 'you kissed me back. So I reckon holding each other close is a good idea.'

It was also a dangerous one. But she couldn't for the life of her think of a reasonable argument. Probably, she admitted silently, because she liked having his arm round her.

Back at the car, he put the basket and picnic blanket into the back of his car and she gave him back his earbud.

'How long did it take you to make that playlist?' she asked.

'Quite a while,' he said. 'I tried to find some really recent stuff, so it wouldn't make you think of Simon or me think of Anna— but I think I must be officially heading for middle age, because none of the chart stuff worked for me.'

She grinned. 'You're thirty-seven and I'm two years younger. We don't *quite* count as middle-aged.'

'Yeah, well. I played it safe and went for the stuff that was around when we were students,' he said.

'I liked it,' she said. 'Dancing to slow songs

from the kind of artists I'd sing to in the car when I'm out on the way to a client.'

'And it's a little more fun than singing "Old MacDonald Had a Farm" for the gazillionth time,' he said.

'E-I-E-I-O,' she retorted, and he laughed.

And that made things easy between them again, breaking the tension. It stopped Jenny wondering what would happen if she slid her arms round his neck and kissed him again—because right now they couldn't take this anywhere and they'd simply have to stop. It made James safe again, which she was pretty sure was a good thing.

As usual, when he dropped Jenny home, James went indoors with her to say hello to her mum and their neighbour Sheila. He showed them the video he'd taken of the waterfall.

'I'd love to see the falls again,' Betty said wistfully. 'But I don't think I'd manage to walk there now.'

'I'll find a wheelchair-accessible waterfall in the Dales and take you,' he promised, and Jenny knew he'd keep that promise. Because James Madden *cared*.

She didn't see him over the weekend, though she knew he'd be up to his eyes organ-

ising Tilly's birthday for the following weekend. But it warmed her that he made the time
to text her with a link to the official web page
for Cotter Falls.

There's a path for pushchairs and wheelchairs.
Maybe we can all go there for a walk, the
weekend after Tilly's birthday?

That would be lovely, she replied.

And you and Betty are very welcome to come
to Tilly's birthday party next Saturday, if you're
not busy and don't mind ten lively pre-schoolers running round. My parents and my sister
will be here, too. Starts at three, but come at
twelve and have lunch with us.

Jenny was pretty sure he was inviting her
as his friend and colleague. And that meant
she could accept the invitation, with pleasure.

On Tuesday morning, James was called out
to see three orphaned lambs.

'I'm glad you're here while the kids are out,'
Joanne Foster said. 'If I'm right, this is going
to break their hearts.'

The Fosters had been farming longer than

James had been a vet, so he was pretty sure Joanne's assessment of her lambs was right. 'Talk me through it,' James said.

'We had three orphans, this year—one of them, the mum rejected her; another of the ewes just didn't have enough milk for her lamb; and we lost the mum of the third one and I couldn't get any of the other ewes to take the lamb on,' Joanne explained. 'We've been bottle-feeding the three of them on formula. The kids have been doing feeds before school, after school and just before bed, I've done the midday feeds, and the lambs were doing well. We had a pen in the barn for them with nice fresh bedding and a heater, and they've had plenty of cuddles and socialisation because the kids' friends have all wanted to come and spend time here.'

'Did any of the lambs get colostrum?' James asked. This was the fluid that the ewes produced just before their milk came in, and was full of important antibodies and minerals.

She nodded. 'The biggest one did—the one whose mum didn't have enough milk.'

'It might be worth taking a tiny bit of colostrum from each ewe and freezing it in an ice cube tray, in future,' James said, 'in case you need it later in the lambing season.'

'I wish we'd done that this year,' Joanne said. 'Because I think our little orphans have got coccidiosis.'

Coccidia was a single-celled parasite that infected nearly all lambs and peaked when they started to eat grass at the age of five to six weeks. Only two of the eleven different types of coccidia were a problem, and they tended to affect lambs with lowered immunity—often bottle-fed lambs who hadn't had the antibodies in their mother's milk to protect them. The parasites damaged the lining of the lamb's gut so the lambs didn't get enough nutrition from their milk.

'You've noticed weight loss and scouring?' James asked.

Joanne nodded. 'And, if you pop your finger in their mouth, they're cold.'

James knew the old shepherd's trick; with young lambs, if the mouth was warm they were OK, but if it was cold they needed more calories.

'How are the rest of your lambs doing?' he asked.

'Fine,' she said. 'We make sure the creep feeders are moved every day to prevent the build-up of infection.' Creep feeders were feeders that the lambs could access easily but the grown sheep couldn't. 'We've grazed the late lambs on different pasture to the early lambs, and there's a low density of lambs.'

'Sounds like perfect hygiene to me,' James said, 'though I think it'll be a good idea to give all the lambs oral drench to combat the infection.'

'You're right,' she said. 'I'll get some in.'

When James saw the orphan lambs in their pen in the barn, it was clear that one of them was really poorly; she was bleeding slightly from the mouth.

'Jo, I'm sorry. I could treat her, but I'm pretty sure this little one's not going to make it and we need to do the kind thing,' he said.

She blinked away tears. 'Sorry. I've been around sheep all my life. I should be used to this.'

James gave her a hug. 'Nobody ever gets used to this. It's the bit of my job I really hate. I can give the other two antibiotics, and they should pull through. But this little one's too poorly.'

'She wasn't bleeding when I called you,' Joanne said. 'I'd never let any of my sheep suffer.'

'I know you wouldn't.'

'James—I can't bear the usual way of euthanising lambs. Not for my little orphan girl,' she said quietly.

He nodded. 'I'll use an injection so she just goes to sleep. Can you weigh her for me so I can get the right dose?'

'Yes,' she said, her voice breaking.

He sorted out the antibiotics for the two bigger lambs; Joanne weighed the littlest one, then sat on the straw with the lamb on her lap.

'She's six kilos,' she said.

'All right.' James prepared the injection and euthanised the lamb while Jo held her close.

'My poor little Buffy,' Joanne said, stroking the lamb while tears slid down her cheeks. 'Dreadful names the kids gave them. Fluffy, Buffy and Puffy.' She stroked the lamb. 'They've been doing video diaries about them at school. They'll be in bits when I break the news to them.'

Just like Joanne herself was in bits, now. Whoever said that farmers were hard-hearted, James thought, didn't have a clue. Even though death was part of every flock cycle, every death was felt—and orphan lambs were always mourned hardest.

His mood was still sombre by the time he got back to the practice.

'Are you OK, James?' Halley asked when he walked into the staff kitchen.

'No. Jo Foster's orphaned lambs have coccidiosis and the littlest one didn't make it,' he said. 'She's really upset, and her kids will be devastated when they get home and learn what's happened.'

Jenny, overhearing the last bit, came over and gave him a brief hug. 'Sounds like a rough morning. I'll stick the kettle on.'

'Mum was going to have one of the lambs at the Children's Farm,' Halley said. 'I'll let her know what's happened. She'll give Jo a ring.'

'I think she needs a listening ear, right now.' James headed for the cookie tin. 'And I need comfort food. I hate this bit of our job.'

'We all do. But think of it another way,' Jenny said. 'That little lamb was poorly and in pain. You saved her from any more suffering.'

'That still doesn't help,' James said. 'I might have to go to the Farleys on the way home and have a cuddle with Sir Woofalot and Cookie, before I pick Tilly up from Mum's.'

'Good idea,' Jenny said. 'Your mum's calling her pup Cookie, then?'

He nodded. 'Their official names are Farley Swale and Farley Ribble—the whole litter's named after rivers. But Cookie's a sensible name—short, and something you wouldn't mind calling across the park.'

'Indeed.' Jenny's mouth twitched. 'Maybe you can talk Tilly into thinking of something a little simpler to call her pup.'

'My daughter is the princess of stubbornness, once her mind's made up about something,' James said with a sigh. 'He'll probably end up answering to Woofy, and over time we can maybe change that to Woody. I can't imagine her calling him Sir Woofalot when she's a grumpy teen.'

'No.' Jenny laughed. 'But the main thing is, he'll always be loved.'

'Like those little orphaned lambs.' He blew out a breath. 'Sorry. I'm not being professional.'

'You're human, James,' Jenny said. 'I'd be the same, in your shoes.'

'And me,' Halley agreed.

It took three biscuits, two cups of tea and a pile of paperwork to settle James before afternoon surgery, and the Farleys were sympathetic when he phoned to ask if he could pop in to see the pups on his way home.

'Saying goodbye to a stock animal is almost as hard as saying goodbye to a pet,' Susan Farley said, handing him a mug of tea, when he told her about how much his morning had upset him. 'And it's worse when it's a baby you've been hand-rearing. I know how I'd feel if we lost one of our calves. Poor Jo must be in bits. And the kids.'

James nodded. 'As a vet, I'm supposed to be detached. But some cases really...' He had to swallow hard to dislodge the lump in his throat. 'I kind of needed a litter of puppies romping over me to cheer me up before I pick Tilly up. I don't want her realising I'm upset and I definitely don't want to explain why.'

'That's what makes you a good vet. You *care*.' Susan patted his arm. 'You're welcome here any time. And I bet your lass will be thrilled to bits when her pup comes home. Does she know her gran's having one of the pups?'

'That's a secret, too, right now,' James said. 'Mum's going to look after Sir Woof-alot while I'm at work and Tilly's at school. Two springer pups.' He groaned. 'It's going to be utter chaos.'

'That's the best kind of chaos in the world,' Susan said with a grin.

The following weekend was Tilly's birthday. She was up early on the Saturday morning, too excited about her party to sleep. And she was thrilled to bits with the pink bicycle James had bought for her and hidden in the garage, wrapped in brown paper and tied up with a bright pink ribbon. His parents had bought her a pink cycling helmet, knee and elbow pads to go with it, as well as training wheels and every pink cycle accessory that a four-year-old could possibly dream of, and she thoroughly enjoyed pedalling her new bicycle up and down the pavement with James at her side.

Jenny and Betty arrived in time for lunch, with special birthday cupcakes iced in pink and with candles to blow out. 'I know your gran has made you a proper cake for your party, but I thought you might like these with your lunch—because you can never have too many candles on your birthday,' Jenny said with a smile.

Tilly was thrilled to bits with the parcel Jenny gave her, wrapped in iridescent pink paper and tied with a white chiffon ribbon. 'Daddy! Look, fairy wings!' she said in delight as she opened the parcel. 'And a fairy crown. And...' Her eyes widened as she saw the magic wand.

'Let me switch that on for you,' Jenny said. 'Now wave it and see what happens.'

The star at the end of the wand lit up, and there was a magic 'twinkling' sound that made Tilly beam her head off and do a magic spell for everyone.

Jenny really paid attention to detail, James thought. She'd chosen exactly the kind of wrapping that Tilly loved, the perfect present…and she'd even hand-drawn the birthday card, a picture of Sir Woofalot that he recognised from a phone snap he'd sent to his mum and she'd clearly shared it with Jenny.

'Daddy, look at my card! It's just like the puppy I want!' Tilly hugged Jenny. 'Thank you! I love it. I love you, too.'

James stilled, panic flaring through him. Would that declaration make Jenny back away?

But Jenny simply hugged the little girl back. 'I love you, too, Tilly. It's always good to tell your friends you love them.'

He thought that message was probably for him rather than for Tilly, a suspicion that was confirmed when she met his gaze and smiled.

Of course she wasn't going to back away from the little girl, even if this thing between them didn't develop the way he'd like it to. She'd said from the start that they'd be friends, and she wouldn't let his daughter or her mother be collateral damage.

'You doing OK?' she asked gently.

There was a lump in his throat. She'd remembered how this day would be bittersweet for him. All he could do was nod.

'OK. But if it gets tough and you need a break at any point, give me the nod and I'll get the girls singing or playing,' she said.

'Thank you,' he said, meaning it from the bottom of his heart. It felt so good to have someone so in tune with his feelings. Jenny Sutton was incredibly special, he thought.

They settled Betty in a comfortable chair in the garden. After lunch, Jenny helped him make the sandwiches with a heart-shaped cutter, and they set up everything in the fridge so all they'd have to do when it was time for the party tea was take everything to the table in the garden. The party bags were all ready on the kitchen dresser, along with a 'Pass the Parcel', stickers, and larger prizes for the main winner of each game.

The weather was perfect, sunny but not too hot, and the garden soon filled with a dozen pre-schoolers and their mums.

Tilly gratefully accepted the presents that her friends had brought to the party.

'She's going to open them after the party,' James explained, 'so she'll have time to enjoy them properly—I know she can't wait to play party games with you all.'

He started off with songs, with a little help from Jenny and his sister Vicky. The girls were all excited and threw themselves in to doing the actions for 'The Wheels on the Bus', 'Heads, Shoulders, Knees and Toes' and 'If You're Happy and You Know It'.

He put Betty and his mother in charge of the music for musical statues. 'Everyone needs to dance,' he said, 'and when the music stops you need to strike a pose.' He demonstrated a silly, gangling pose, and all the little girls laughed. 'Nobody's out,' he said. 'Betty and Christine will choose the person with the best pose in each round, and that person will get a sticker.'

'Yay!' the little girls yelled.

Once everyone had won a sticker and the overall winner had won a sparkly hairband, James put on a green bucket hat that had been customised with a woolly sheep glued onto it, and explained the rules of Simon the Sheep Says. 'So if I say "Simon the Sheep Says", you do what I say,' he said. 'And if I don't say "Simon the Sheep Says," then you stand still. And if you get it wrong, you'll get a sticker. The last person to get a sticker wins.'

Jenny was a great help, whispering ideas to him, and the little girls were soon quacking like a duck, hopping like a bunny, waving their right hands or walking like an elephant. The prize for the winner of this game was a rainbow bangle, and the girls were clearly having a wonderful time.

After some more dancing, they played a few rounds of 'Duck, Duck, Goose'; and then it was time for the birthday tea.

'I think I've got them all a bit too excited,' James said. 'They're never going to sit down for tea and birthday cake.'

'Leave this to me,' Jenny said with a smile. 'Everyone, we're going to play "Sleeping Lions". Do you know how to play it?'

'No,' the girls chorused.

James had never heard of it, either.

'Everyone has to lie down,' Jenny said. 'I'm going to walk round, and anyone who wriggles or giggles is out—you'll get a sticker, if you're out, and you have to help me wake the lions by telling a joke. And the winner is the one who can stay still the longest without wriggling or giggling. Who's going to be my most sleepy lion?'

'Me!' the little girls yelled. 'Me! Me!'

But then Jenny put her finger to her lips. 'Shh! The lions are sleepy,' she said in a loud whisper, and they all lay down and were all still. There were wriggles and giggles, and lots of shushing, but eventually everyone had a sticker and the chance to tell a joke, and the winner ended up being presented with a pink hair scrunchie.

This was just the sort of thing that Anna would've done, James thought—knowing how to calm little girls down and get them ready for the birthday tea party.

Meanwhile Vicky and Christine had quietly ferried out the plates of sandwiches, mini sausage rolls, cherry tomatoes, carrot sticks and crisps from the kitchen to the low tables James had set out.

It had been a long time since Jenny had been to a child's birthday party. She could see that Tilly was having a wonderful time with her friends; the little girl's face was bright pink and full of smiles.

Once the girls were all seated, Jenny went round with a jug of juice, filling everyone's cup. The mums helped, too, passing plates of food and making sure that everyone had something to eat. Jenny was pleased that they chatted to her as if she was one of them, even though she didn't have a child at the party; she knew them all either from their own school-days or as a client at the practice.

If things had been different, she and Simon could've hosted birthday parties like these... Except she knew Simon would've hated every minute of it, whereas James had seemed to be enjoying himself as much as the children were.

When the girls had finished the savouries, Jenny helped Christine bring out the dishes, ice cream and bowls of toppings, and the mums helped the girls make their own ice-cream sundae with sprinkles, strawberries, raspberries and a chocolate flake.

Finally, they cleared the table. Jenny took her phone from her pocket and filmed James lighting the candles on the bright pink birth-day cake, and then everyone singing 'Happy Birthday to You'.

'Take a deep breath, and make a wish inside your head when you blow out the candles,' James told Tilly.

She did so and blew out all the candles, while her friends clapped and cheered.

Christine took the cake back to the kitchen, ready to be sliced, wrapped and slipped into the party bags, while Jenny and Vicky got the girls playing pass the parcel and then another game of 'Musical Statues', where this time the girls had to do an animal pose when the music stopped.

Finally, the party was over. James helped Tilly to give out the party bags as her friends went home, then finally flopped into a garden chair.

'That,' he said, 'was exhausting.'

'But huge fun,' Vicky said. 'It feels like for ever since mine were that small. You forget what they're like at that age. So sweet and full of fun. When they get to ten, the boys only want to play football or video games.'

The next day, James and Tilly popped round to Jenny's with a huge bouquet of flowers. 'We just wanted to say thank you for everything you did yesterday,' he said.

'No problem. That's what friends do,' she said.

The problem was, she was starting to think that she wanted more than friendship from him. But how could she offer him anything when she knew her mother would need more of her time and attention as the months went on?

CHAPTER EIGHT

ON SUNDAY, James dropped Tilly over to his mother's so he could check that he had all the bits of puppy paraphernalia he needed for their spaniel and make sure that the house and garden were puppy proof without Tilly asking questions. He secured wire netting to the wrought-iron garden gate so the pup wouldn't be able to squeeze through or under it, and planned distractions so she wouldn't notice. On Monday, after work, he drove his parents and Tilly to pick up Farley Ribble and Farley Swale—better known as Sir Woofalot and Cookie—from the farm and took them all back to his parents' house.

Tilly was beside herself with joy, having two puppies to play with, and he noticed that his mum was smiling. Clearly having pattering paws and waggy tails in the house again was helping to stop her missing Treacle so much.

Both Tilly and Sir Woofalot fell asleep in the car on the way back to the cottage. James woke them both so Sir Woofalot could go out into the garden to start his bedtime routine of having a wee, and Tilly could clean her teeth, then tucked his daughter up in bed with the pup cuddled up next to her. He read them stories until Tilly fell asleep with the pup in her arms. He couldn't resist taking a picture of them together and using it as his phone's lock screen. Cuteness personified, he thought.

But they'd agreed that the pup would sleep in the kitchen, so he gently disentangled the pup and took him downstairs, before sending photos to his sister and to Jenny.

Vicky texted back.

Mum looks so happy. We should've talked her into this before. Have a good first night with Sir Woofalot—hope he doesn't live up to his name! xx

James took a selfie of the pup asleep on his lap and sent it back to both her and to Jenny.

Sir Sleepalot, I hope. x

Jenny texted back.

Gorgeous! Have a good first night x

He suppressed the wish that she was here to share it with him. That wasn't their deal. He suppressed the sudden wave of loneliness, too. He couldn't possibly be lonely, not with his daughter and a tiny puppy to fill his time. And yet he was. He and Jenny had agreed to be friends, but dancing with her by the waterfalls and kissing her had thrown him for a loop and made him realise just how much he missed sharing his life with another adult.

How was he going to persuade her that this thing between them could work—that they could have time for each other as well as looking after Tilly and her mum?

'You're the walking epitome of the owner of a new puppy,' Archer said when James walked into the practice on Tuesday morning.

Jenny had to agree. There were dark shadows under his eyes, and she had to resist the urge to smooth his hair and stroke his cheek. 'How much sleep did you get?' she asked.

'Not very much,' James admitted. 'I bought one of those special teddies for him with a heated pad and a ticking sound to remind him of his mum's heartbeat—but it didn't seem to work. He woke five times last night and cried.'

'And you went down to him each time, so he's learned that howling gets him attention,' Archer said, tutting. 'Bet he ends up sleeping on your bed.'

'No, he won't, and I've told Tilly he can't sleep on her bed, either.' James yawned. 'I need coffee.'

'Try putting the radio on, tonight,' Jenny said. 'So you get the white noise between the stations. That might help him settle.'

'You,' James said, 'live with a cat. I'm not taking puppy advice from *you*.'

Halley came in to hear the last bit, and laughed. 'Oh, dear. New pup-owner all grumpy from lack of sleep, are we?'

'Just you wait. Babies are worse than puppies,' he grumbled.

'Your Tilly's an angel, and you know it,' Halley teased.

'Huh,' James said, and made everyone a hot drink. Jenny noticed that he put twice as much coffee as normal in his own mug and added enough cold water that he could drink it straight down. 'I have patients waiting,' he said.

Jenny couldn't help it. She gave a soft puppy

howl, and he groaned, leaving the staff kitchen to gales of laughter from his colleagues.

At lunchtime, James still had shadows under his eyes.

'Here.' She made him a mug of coffee.

'Thanks.' He took it gratefully. 'Would you like to bring your mum over to meet the puppies on Thursday evening? At my mum's place—stay for dinner.'

She raised an eyebrow at him. 'It's a bit rude to invite myself over with no notice—and to invite myself for dinner.'

'It was Mum's suggestion,' he said. 'She told me you were lovely with her when she had to say goodbye to Treacle.'

'It's the hardest bit of being a pet owner. Of course I'd be kind,' Jenny said.

But on Thursday evening she duly took her mum over to Christine's house, along with a bottle of wine and a bunch of flowers.

'Oh, they're wonderful,' Betty said, making a fuss of the puppies.

Tilly was beyond excited, and was carefully teaching the pups to sit. 'This is puppy nursery school, like my school,' she told them, offering them a tiny slice of cocktail sausage when they sat nicely. 'You'll go to big puppy school next.'

Village hall, James mouthed to Jenny, and she knew exactly who was running the puppy training classes.

It was incredibly charming, watching Tilly with the pups; she was gentle and sweet, and so like her father that it made Jenny's heart squeeze.

Particularly when she realised that, actually, she *did* want a child.

A child like Tilly.

She wanted Tilly—*and* Tilly's dad.

Not that she was going to pressure James by telling him how she felt. They'd agreed that they'd just see how things went. No risks, no worries.

On Sunday afternoon, James picked Jenny and Betty up and drove them out to Cotter Falls. He ended up pushing Betty's wheelchair while Tilly skipped along, holding Jenny's hand and chattering to her about the waterfall.

Betty was really grateful. 'I can't remember the last time I came here. I miss—' She shook her head as the word escaped her, but James knew what she meant. She missed having freedom to go wherever she wanted instead of having to rely on a chair when she got tired. 'You're so thoughtful, James.'

'I always keep my promises,' he said. 'I would never make a promise that I have no intention of keeping.'

She nodded. 'You're a good man.'

It was good to know that she approved of him. But her daughter was the one he needed to persuade to give him a chance.

On the way back, they stopped at James' parents' house so Tilly could show off the new tricks Sir Woofalot had learned, offering his paw for a treat and sitting nicely when she asked.

'Shall we take him out for a walk, Tilly?' he asked.

Jenny felt her eyes widening. As a vet, of course he'd know that puppies were vulnerable to infections until a couple of weeks after the second lot of vaccinations, so they weren't advised to go out for walks until then.

As if he'd guessed her thoughts, James said, 'Socialising is good for him, and his feet won't be touching the ground.' He picked up a baby sling he'd customised for the pup, settling the spaniel into the sling so he was safely cuddled against James's chest.

They looked unbelievably cute together, and Jenny's heart felt as if it had done a somersault. 'Let me take a picture of this for your mum and your sister,' she said.

And the fact it would be on her phone so she'd be able to keep it had nothing to do with anything, she told herself.

'I'll stay here while you youngsters go out,' Betty said, 'if you don't mind, Christine.'

'I'm glad you're staying with us,' James's mum said, 'because I'd like to ask your opinion about a new cake recipe I tried today—I can't work out what's missing. Let's have a cup of tea and you can try the cake and tell me what you think.'

Jenny loved the fact that James's family were so inclusive, making her mum feel part of them. Christine was a few years younger than Betty and much more mobile, but she treated Betty as a valued equal rather than as an object of pity, and Jenny appreciated that.

They walked into the village, with Tilly holding Jenny's hand. Various people were sitting at tables outside the pub and Sally's café, and waved at James and Jenny in acknowledgement. James let Tilly introduce the pup to everyone he knew, and Sir Woofalot thoroughly enjoyed having a fuss made of him.

'Are you and James…?' Sally asked, outside the café.

Jenny smiled, hoping that she could stop this particular bit of village gossip before it spooked James. 'We're friends and colleagues. Tilly's a sweetheart. And who can resist taking a new puppy out for a bit of socialisation?'

'Not me,' Sally agreed, and went to make a fuss of the spaniel.

On Monday morning, Cally Bywater brought her fourteen-year-old cat in to the surgery.

'He's not eaten for the last twenty-four hours, so I know he's not right, and this morning he was sick,' she told James. 'I don't like the way he's miaowing. I think he's in pain.'

James had seen from the file that Boots had a history of pancreatitis but managed well with dietary management. It was possible that this was a flare-up, but it might be something else.

'Let me examine him,' he said.

The cat was salivating much more than usual. James checked his temperature, which was on the low side, and when he examined Boots the cat clearly had a tender abdomen.

'I'd like to admit him for some investigations, to see if it's his pancreatitis flaring up or if there's a new problem,' James said. 'I'll check his bloods and give him some pain relief and fluids, and then tomorrow if he's well enough we'll sedate him and give him an X-ray to see what's going on.'

'I know he's getting on a bit,' Cally said, 'but he's been well up until this week.' Her voice wobbled. 'I'm not ready to say good-bye yet.'

'Hopefully it won't come to that,' James reassured her. 'And in the meantime we'll keep him comfortable.'

'Thank you.'

She was clearly close to tears, and he patted her arm. 'Try not to worry. I know that's an easy thing to say, because he's been part of your life for years.'

'He was a rescue kitten,' she said, 'my twenty-first present from my mum—and Mum's not with us any more. I can't lose him yet.' She blinked back the tears. 'I just want him well and happy and back with my family.'

'I'll do what I can,' James promised.

When she left, James took a blood sample from Boots. 'Let's get you comfortable, boy,' he said, and gave the cat some pain relief along with anti-sickness medication. He took the cat to the kennel area in the back, making a fuss of him.

'Is that Cally Bywater's Boots?' Jenny asked, coming in.

'Yes. Actually, I could do with your help,' James said. 'Have you got ten minutes?'

'I can make the time,' Jenny said.

'Thanks. He's been sick and he's not eating, plus he's hyper-salivating. I've just given him some pain relief and anti-emetics, but I need to get some fluids into him. Tomorrow, if he's perked up, we'll sedate him and do an X-ray to see if it's his pancreatitis or something else.'

'What do his bloods say?' Jenny asked.

'I've just given them to Halley,' he said. 'I'll tell you in a few minutes when she's run them through.'

Jenny sat on a chair, and cuddled the cat. 'I assume we're giving him subcutaneous fluids?' she asked.

James nodded. They both knew that putting some fluids underneath a cat's skin, where it could be gradually absorbed into the body, was a good way of getting fluids into a dehydrated cat; and most cats tolerated it really well.

He set up the hanger for the drip, put the bag of electrolyte solution on the hanger, then swiftly got the fluid set in place, checking the tubing to make sure there were no blockage or leaks.

'Are you sitting comfortably?' he asked, knowing it would take ten minutes or so for the fluids to be administered.

'Ready,' she said, stroking the top of Boots's head. 'We're doing all right, aren't we, Boots?'

Gently, James picked up a loose roll of skin above the cat's right shoulder blade and inserted the needle into the tented space between the skin folds, all the while talking to the cat while Jenny soothed him, then adjusted the lock on the fluid set so the electrolyte solution gradually came through.

Once it was done, he removed the needle and discarded it safely in the sharps bin.

'Well done, little man,' James said. 'Let's get you comfortable, and hopefully you'll feel a bit better by this afternoon.'

When the cat was settled, he checked the blood results. 'ALT's high and potassium's low,' he said to Jenny.

'So at this stage it could be pancreatitis or possibly an infection,' Jenny said. 'You said he'd been vomiting and not eating, so that's probably why his potassium's low.'

'We'll give him some potassium in with the

next lot of fluids,' James said. 'That'll help with the hypersalivation, too.'

The next day, Boots seemed a lot brighter; he was better hydrated and hadn't vomited again.

Jenny did the sedation while James did the X-ray.

'It looks like severe pancreatitis to me,' he said. 'But Boots also has gallstones, and they're partly blocking his bile ducts. No wonder he's been in pain, poor boy.' He grimaced. 'He's fourteen and he's had a good life. I know Cally's not ready to say goodbye, but I'm not sure I'd want to put him through surgery. Maybe the kindest thing would be to let him not wake up.'

'But he's been well until recently, and he's stable,' Jenny argued. 'You could remove his gall bladder, and feed him by tube for a few days until he's able to eat properly again. He'll pull through.'

'Maybe,' James said. 'I'll have a word with Cally and see what she wants us to do.'

He came back from the phone call. 'She's asked us to do the surgery,' he said. 'I've told her I'll need to remove his gall bladder, and he'll be here for a few days so we can feed him by tube to make sure he gets the right nutrients while he's recovering from his operation. We can give him his meds that way, too; it'll be less stressful for him.'

Jenny deepened the sedation to full anaesthesia and James worked swiftly, taking out the gall bladder and the stones obstructing the bile tract. Once he'd sewed up, he fitted a nasogastric feeding tube through Boots's nose, and protected it with a dressing.

Jenny brought the cat round and gave him a cuddle, while James called Cally to let her know that Boots was round from the anaesthetic and doing OK, and he'd call her tomorrow after morning surgery with an update.

On Wednesday, Boots was definitely starting to perk up and ate a little bit of fish on his own. He was still being fed mainly by tube, but he was clearly more comfortable.

'Can you text with me an update, tomorrow?' Jenny asked. 'I know we're not supposed to have favourites, but...'

'Of course I will,' James said.

But on Thursday evening, just before James put Tilly to bed, he was called out to the Davidsons' farm; they had a cow in stage two of labour, but she wasn't progressing.

James called his mum to let her know the

situation. 'I don't know how long it'll take,' he said.

'Bring Tilly and Sir Woofalot here,' Christine said. 'They can have a sleepover.'

'Thanks, Mum.' Though he had a feeling that he'd need a hand with this particular case. On the way to the farm from his parents', he tried to get hold of Archer but the senior partner wasn't around. Feeling guilty, he called Jenny. 'Sorry, I know this isn't fair because you don't work on Thursdays, but I can't get hold of Archer and I have a funny feeling about this. Lee Davidson knows what he's doing, so if he's called me for help there's a chance it's really serious. I might need to do a section. Could you help?'

'I'll get Sheila next door to sit with Mum, if need be,' Jenny said. 'Call me when you get to the farm and you've had time to assess the cow.'

'It's her third calf, and she hasn't had a problem in previous calvings,' Lee, the farmer, told James. 'I think this calf is a big one.'

James checked; the calf was big and the cow's cervix was tight. The calf was viable, but she definitely needed help.

'How long has she been in labour?' he asked.

'Early hours of this morning,' Lee said.

'I could give her an epidural and we can try traction again, or we can do a section,' James said.

'I'm not taking any risks with my Heather,' Lee said scratching the cow's poll. 'Let's get the calf out of the side.'

'I'm calling Jenny in to give me a hand,' James said, and did so. Then he gowned up, gave the cow a local anaesthetic to keep her comfortable and then slid the big needle in for the vertebral spinal block. He gave the cow an anti-inflammatory as well.

Heather mooed. She was clearly still having contractions, but the calf wasn't moving.

By the time James had prepared the surgical field, shaving the cow's hair away from her skin, Jenny was there, scrubbed up and gloved.

'We're going in on the left flank,' James said. The cow was haltered to a ring in the wall, and her tail was tied loosely to a rear leg to keep it out of the way of surgery.

James checked that the anaesthetic had reached an adequate level and scratched her poll. 'You're a good girl, Heather. We're going to help you with your baby,' he said. He looked at Lee Davidson. 'She's more relaxed now. We can make a start.'

He used scrub and surgical spirit on the surgical area, then made the vertical skin incision before cutting through the muscle layers, careful not to damage the rumen.

'I've got a calf leg,' he said as he explored Heather's abdomen. 'Ready to do the uterine incision. Can you two pull the calf out for me?'

He made sure the incision was big enough so the calf could be extracted safely, and got two of the calf's legs out. 'I need one of you on legs and one supporting the calf as it comes out,' he said.

'I'll do the support—you do the legs, Lee,' Jenny said.

Under James's direction, Lee pulled the calf out and Jenny supported the calf so there wasn't any strain on the incision, and then Jenny attended to the calf.

'It's a girl,' she said. She cleaned the membranes off the calf's face so she could breathe, then put her elbows underneath her, sitting her like a frog so her pelvis was square. 'This puts a bit less pressure on the lungs,' she told Lee. 'The calf's doing well, James.'

James closed the uterus with Jenny's help, washed out the incision with saline solution and sewed up the muscle layers and skin, then finally gave the cow some antibiotics and sprayed the incision with silver spray to minimise the risk of infection.

Lee stripped some colostrum from the dam and tube-fed the calf, then gave Heather a good drink.

When he placed the calf with her mum for bonding, the calf tried to stand, wobbled a bit and fell back into the soft straw.

Heather mooed and went over to her, sniffed her, licked her, and the calf stood.

'That's brilliant,' James said. 'I love this moment.'

'Me, too,' Jenny said, hugging him.

He enjoyed her warmth and closeness, the moment of joy when a new life had just begun. And, when she pulled back, he missed that closeness.

They said goodbye to Lee, leaving him to check on the cow and the calf, and headed for their cars.

'I need to decompress,' James said. 'Come back to my place for a cup of tea? Tilly and the pup are at Mum's tonight, because I wasn't sure how long I'd be and I didn't want to keep Mum out half the night.'

Back to his place.

Where they'd be alone.

This might not be a good idea. They were both emotional, and probably shouldn't be on their own together—especially after that kiss by the waterfall.

But, at the same time, he had a point; she needed to decompress before she went home. They didn't do that many caesarean sections on cows, and there was always the worry with a complicated delivery that a calf might not make it.

'All right,' she said.

She followed him home and parked in the street outside his cottage; he waited for her by the front door.

'There's a clean towel in the downstairs cloakroom if you want to wash your hands and arms,' he said.

She smiled, knowing that despite changing out of her scrubs she still smelled of cow. 'Thank you.'

When she came out, he'd clearly washed his own hands and arms at the kitchen sink because he was putting a hand towel into the washing machine.

'That's better,' he said. 'Thanks for coming out and helping, tonight.'

'I wouldn't have missed it for the world,' she said. 'It's so special, seeing new-born calves wobbling over to their mums.'

'Isn't it just?' He switched on the kettle and threw a couple of teabags into two mugs.

'Tsk. My mother would tell you to warm the teapot and do it properly,' she said, teasing him.

'Properly, hmm?'

Then she realised he was looking at her mouth, and all of a sudden her stomach swooped. She found herself looking at his mouth, too. Remembering what it had felt like, against hers…

She wasn't sure which of them moved first, but then she was in his arms, the kettle and the tea forgotten. He nibbled her lower lip, and she opened her mouth to let him deepen the kiss. Eyes closed, all she was aware of was the warmth of his lips against hers, the steady thump of his heartbeat, his clean male scent. And it just wasn't enough. She wanted more.

He broke the kiss and drew a trail of kisses down the side of her neck, making her shiver and tip her head back.

'Jenny,' he whispered against her collarbone. 'We shouldn't be doing this.'

She knew. But, for the life of her, she couldn't marshal her common sense and tell him to stop. The words that came out of her mouth came from a deeper place. 'I don't care.'

'Jenny.' Her name sounded hoarse, as if it had been ripped from him. 'Tell me to stop.'

'I don't want you to stop,' she said.

He pulled back and looked her straight in the eye. 'You sure about that?'

No. It was utterly insane. 'Yes.'

He drew her back into his arms, kissed her, then scooped her up and carried her up the stairs.

Even Simon hadn't swept her off her feet like this, and it made her feel all fluttery.

He set her back on her feet outside the door she knew led to his bedroom.

'Just so you know,' he said quietly, 'I've never shared this bed with anyone.'

He was telling her that there were no memories of Anna. That he knew exactly who was going to be in his bed, and he wasn't pretending she was someone else.

'Thank you,' she said. 'That's…' She swallowed the lump in her throat.

'It's been a while for me,' he said. 'Just as I'm guessing it's been a while for you.'

She nodded.

'No expectations. No pressure. But right now I want you so badly, I can hardly see straight.'

'That makes two of us,' she said, and stepped back into his arms.

He kissed her; then he opened the door and led her inside.

'I'm at the back of the house,' he said, 'and nobody can see in. But if you want me to shut the curtains…'

She shook her head. The soft, gentle light filtering into the room was perfect.

'Kiss me, Jenny,' he said.

She reached up, slid her hands round the back of his neck and drew his head down to hers. He was trembling, she noticed, guessed he felt as nervous and excited and mixed-up about this as she did.

When she broke the kiss, she stroked his face. 'Sure about this?'

'No. Yes.' He gave her a wry smile. 'I don't want to think with my head, right now.'

'Me neither,' she said.

'Then let's not think. Not talk. Just…'

In answer, she slid her fingers under the hem of her T-shirt and drew it over her head before dropping it on the floor.

He gave a sharp intake of breath. 'You're beautiful.'

She put her finger to his lips. 'You're the one who said no talking.'

He raised his eyebrows at her, sucked the tip of her finger into his mouth, and all the words in her head vanished.

He traced the edge of her bra with the tip of his finger, making her breathing quicken, and then stroked his way up her spine and unhooked her bra. With shaking hands, she grasped the hem of his T-shirt and pulled it upwards. His shoulders were broad and his chest was muscular—from his work rather than from the gym—and there was a light sprinkling of dark hair across his chest. His abdomen was flat, and she couldn't resist tracing one finger down the arrowing of hair.

My turn, he mouthed, and cupped her breasts, rubbing the pads of his thumbs across her hardening nipples.

But touching wasn't enough.

Even though she didn't say it, maybe it showed on her face, because he dipped his head and took one nipple into his mouth. She gasped and slid her hands into his hair, drawing him closer as he teased her with his lips and his tongue.

He undid the button of her jeans, and then the zip, before sliding the soft denim over her hips.

She shimmied, but they stuck at her knees. Stretch denim might be great for work, when you had to bend and stretch while you dealt with animals, but they were the worst clothing in the world when you wanted to remove them quickly.

'Let me give you a hand,' he said, and dropped to his knees in front of her. He nuzzled her abdomen, sending sparks of desire through her, and gently tugged the denim down. She stood on one leg, letting him pull the material over one ankle, then the other.

He pressed a kiss to her inner thigh, then rose to his feet. 'I'm in your hands,' he said.

Her fingers were trembling as she undid the button and zip of his jeans and drew them downwards. His erection was obvious through the soft jersey of his underpants.

This was crazy.

They weren't even dating properly.

But, for the life of her, she couldn't stop. She needed him. Wanted him as much as he wanted her. Seeing the evidence of his arousal made her feel like a goddess, strong and gorgeous.

'Jenny.'

He kissed her again, and time stopped. She had no idea which of them took off which bits of clothing, but the next thing she knew they were in his bed, she was straddling him, and he was looking at her as if she was the most gorgeous woman in the world.

'I have just about enough sense left,' he said, 'to ask you to open the drawer in front of you.'

She felt the colour flood into her face. She hadn't even thought about a condom.

'And it's not because I made assumptions,' he said. 'I knew I was going to look for a partner. It made sense to be—well, sensible about it. Make provisions.' He looked at her. 'If you've changed your mind, all you have to do is say so. I'd never push you into anything.'

She shook her head. 'I just feel stupid that I hadn't thought of it.'

He sat up, and kissed the tip of her nose. 'You've very far from being stupid. We got carried away. Which was entirely my fault.'

'I was with you all the way,' she said, and wriggled slightly against him. 'I don't care if it isn't sensible. If we stop now, I'm going to spontaneously combust.'

'Me, too,' he said, and kissed her again.

She reached over to his drawer for the condom. Helped him slide it on, unsure whose hands were shaking more, his or hers. And then she lowered herself onto him.

Afterwards, they showered together and made love again.

And then they got dressed and he led her downstairs. 'Let me make you that tea.'

'I ought to get back,' she said. 'Sheila's sitting with Mum, and it's not fair to stay out.'

'I know,' he said, 'but stay long enough to have a mug of tea. Just a few minutes. Because I'd really like to sit in the garden with you in my lap and watch the stars come out.'

How could she resist?

They didn't talk about what had just happened between them, just sat at the table on the patio with the mugs of tea in front of them, with her on his lap and his arms wrapped round her, her head resting on his shoulders.

Right at that moment she felt perfectly content—knew this was a moment out of time, that she needed to savour it, but would've been happy for this one moment to last and last and last.

In the distance, they heard the hoot of an owl, and then an answering hoot.

'Oh, that's lovely,' she said. 'It sounds like barn owls. I love it when you see one flying across the fields.'

'Me, too.' He stroked her hair.

The tea sat on the table, untouched, neither of them willing to move away from each other for long enough to pick up a mug.

They heard the owl again and she knew she couldn't stay any longer, much as she wanted to. She kissed him lightly. 'I need to go, James.'

'I wish you didn't, but I'm not going to be unfair.' Reluctantly, he let her slide off his lap; then he walked her to the car and kissed her goodnight. 'Sweet dreams. I'll call you tomorrow.'

James lay in bed, the curtains still open, thinking. He could still smell Jenny's floral scent on his sheets and he wished she was still there beside him, maybe asleep in his arms.

Tonight had changed everything.

But where did they go from here?

Both he and Jenny were wary of things going wrong because of the potential collateral damage to Tilly and Betty. But, the more he thought about it, the more it was obvious that their fears were unfounded. Both Jenny and Betty had taken to Tilly; and his daughter had taken to them, too. He was pretty sure that Betty and Tilly would both be happy for him and Jenny to be more than just friends.

Though the next step would be actually merging their lives…and that would be huge.

And a little voice in his head reminded him that he'd never expected to lose Anna. Could the shockingly unexpected repeat itself? This time, Tilly would be old enough to be hurt…

He shook himself. What had happened to Anna was tragic and incredibly rare. Besides, his relationship with Jenny was still in the early stages. He should be enjoying it instead of worrying and overthinking things.

Once Jenny had thanked Sheila for helping her mum to bed, told her about the new calf arriving safely and said goodnight, she checked on Betty, who was sound asleep, and headed for bed.

Though sleep evaded her.

What had just happened between her and James had been bubbling underneath their friendship for weeks. Their shared kisses, dancing together by the waterfall—it had all led up to that moment, heated up by the urgency of that difficult calving. They'd celebrated the wonder of a new life.

But had they just made a huge mistake?

They couldn't simply please themselves. They had Tilly and Betty to think of. And, although Jenny was pretty sure that Tilly liked both herself and Betty, and she knew that Betty doted on Tilly, merging her life with James's would be an enormous step. Betty's health would continue to decline, and Tilly's needs would change as she grew older. It would be a big ask, for all of them. There would need to be compromises—some of them difficult.

James wasn't like Simon. As her mother had pointed out, he was a family man. He was reliable as a colleague and as a friend. He'd proved himself to be a generous lover, too, wanting to cuddle her afterwards.

If she could make this work with anyone, it would be James.

But.

What if it went wrong? They worked together, too. Everything would come crashing down round her ears.

And, no matter how she tried to shake it, the fear wouldn't go away.

CHAPTER NINE

JAMES AND JENNY spent the next couple of weeks circling round the issue. James was busy with Tilly and Sir Woofalot, and Jenny was busy with Betty. The way the caseloads panned out, James was out on farm visits when Jenny was seeing patients in Burndale Veterinary Surgery, so they barely passed each other at work.

They both knew they were avoiding each other and making excuses not to see each other outside work; and the longer the time went on, the more awkward it felt.

On the Wednesday, they were both in together and had to work together to treat a spaniel who had a grass seed stuck in her ear. The dog had been scratching vigorously and shaking her head, and when Jenny looked in her ear the signs of inflammation were obvious. She could see the grass seed but it was very deep in the spaniel's ear and would be painful to remove. The only solution was sedation.

She needed James to do the anaesthetic while she used an endoscope and tiny tweezers to take out the grass seed, then gave the dog antibiotics and pain relief.

'Thanks for your help,' she said to James.

'Pleasure. It's a good reminder for me to make sure I check Sir Woofalot's ears and paws after every walk.'

She nodded in acknowledgement.

'Are you and Betty busy on Sunday?' he asked.

She paused a fraction too long. Now if she said they were busy he'd know it was a deliberate brush-off, and that wasn't fair. 'I'm not sure,' she said carefully.

'Tilly and I are taking the pup for his first visit to the sea,' he said. 'The plan is to go to Filey, paddle in the sea, make a sandcastle, have fish and chips, and then Woofy and Tilly can both have a nap in the car on the way home.'

It had been a long while since she'd been to the sea. Even longer for her mum, she'd bet.

She blew out a breath. 'James. After…' She

could feel the colour shooting into her face and she couldn't bring herself to say the words *after we made love*. 'It's difficult.'

'It's simple,' he corrected. 'The seaside, a puppy and chips. I'm asking you as Tilly's friend.'

'That's emotional blackmail.'

'It's not meant to be,' he said. 'It's meant to be taking the emotion out of it. An afternoon out, and it'll be fun for all of us, whether it's sunny or it's raining.'

Could it really be that simple?

'Have a think about it,' he said. 'Text me and let me know.'

He'd really messed things up between them, James thought. He'd taken it too far, too fast. He should've stuck to offering Jenny a cup of tea after the calf was born, and nothing more than a cup of tea. Better still, he should've let her go straight home from the Davidsons' farm.

Unlike his own marriage, Jenny's hadn't been entirely happy. She'd been the one to make all the compromises, and Simon had pushed her to her limit. James knew he needed to be fair, now, and back off until she was ready.

Though he didn't want to lose her friendship. He needed to find a way of making that clear to her.

Waiting was torture, but finally on Friday morning she texted him.

Mum and I are delighted to accept your and Tilly's invitation to Sir Woofalot's first trip to the seaside. Let me know what time.

He hadn't realised just how tense he'd got until it felt as if his shoulders had just shed a huge weight.

He replied.

Tilly will be delighted to see Betty. And I'm glad I haven't quite ruined our friendship. Pick you up at half-past nine.

So was he saying that now they were just good friends, and nothing more than that? Jenny wondered. Well, it was what she'd wanted. Safe. So she shouldn't feel disappointed that he was doing what she'd asked.

She typed back.

We'll be ready.

On Sunday, she felt oddly shy with him. He helped her mum into the back seat; Tilly was in the back in her booster seat, and Sir Woof-alot had a harness attachment that clipped to the seatbelt and kept him safely on his blanket, settled between Tilly and Betty.

Jenny's hand accidentally brushed James's as they both put their seatbelts on, and the glance he sent her was loaded with meaning. But they couldn't talk about the situation here, in front of Tilly and Betty. It would have to wait, and she'd have to play this as if she and James were no more than friends.

Despite the worries churning in her head, Jenny enjoyed the drive to the east coast.

'Filey's quite dog-friendly. There's a bit where dogs are forbidden, but a lot where they can go,' he said, 'plus it's good for wheelchairs.'

He parked the car and got Betty's chair out; while she helped Betty into the chair, James got Tilly and the puppy out of the car.

He was strict with Tilly when it came to suncream and hat-wearing, and also gently applied suncream to Betty's face and arms.

'Can I put suncream on your shoulders?' he asked Jenny. 'I don't want you to burn.' Then he added in a lower voice, so only she could hear, 'I'm asking you as your friend.'

Her friend, not her lover. Well, that worked for her. 'Thank you,' she said.

Her mum actually had a paddle in the sea and really enjoyed it, and they all loved watching Sir Woofalot's reaction to the sea. At first, the spaniel backed away, unsure of the swishing movement of the incoming tide; but then Tilly walked into the sea until her ankles were covered in water, and the pup grew braver, trotting by her side with James holding a long lead.

Five minutes later, Sir Woofalot was happily splashing in the shallows with Tilly, under the supervision of James.

Sir Woofalot had a nap on Betty's lap while James, Tilly and Jenny built a sandcastle together, including seaweed that Tilly had collected to decorate the castle and shells to serve as windows. James dug a moat round it, and Jenny helped Tilly to collect buckets of water to put into the moat.

She took a selfie of all of them next to the castle, and then headed back to the promenade with Tilly to get fish and chips while James sat with Betty and Sir Woofalot. The pup sat very nicely and lifted a paw to ask for a flake of fish, which he happily licked from James's hands.

It really was the perfect family day out, Jenny thought.

At the end of the day, the pup was tired, so James put him in the baby sling. 'Oof, pup, your weight must've doubled since last week!' he grumbled, though he was smiling.

'I'm tired, too, Daddy,' Tilly said.

'All right, honey. It's been a busy day. Do you want me to give you a piggyback?' James asked.

'You can sit on my lap if you want, Tilly,' Betty said. 'And then maybe your dad can push both of us.'

James glanced at Jenny, who nodded.

'That's kind, Betty,' James said. 'Thank you.'

'Thank you, Betty,' Tilly said, and climbed onto her lap.

'You can give me a hand pushing, if you like,' he said to Jenny.

She took one of the handles while he took the other, and they pushed the chair back up the ramp to the promenade.

She wasn't quite sure how it happened, but his hand was curled round one of hers on the handle, and it made her heart skip a beat. This felt like being a proper family. Could she—dared she—try to make a family with James and Tilly?

James's fingers were laced through Jenny's. And today had felt like a real family day out. As if they belonged together.

Could he and Jenny make a multi-generational blended family?

He'd always love Anna, but now he was ready to risk his heart again with Jenny. He already knew that Tilly adored Jenny and Betty, and it was mutual; he liked Betty very much; and he was pretty sure that Betty liked him, too.

But how did Jenny feel about him?

He liked her. More than liked her. If he was honest with himself, he'd fallen in love with her common sense, her ready smile, her warmth.

They were friends. They'd been compatible as lovers, too; there was no reason why they couldn't make this work.

Admittedly, life would become more complicated as Betty's health declined and her needs changed, but he was prepared for that. He wanted to support Jenny.

But, given how she'd been let down before,

would Jenny trust him to do that? And how could he make her see that she could trust him?

The following day, James had an invitation to a former colleague from London's fortieth birthday party in York, in a fortnight's time. He persuaded Jenny to go with him as his plus one; Tamsin agreed to keep Betty company, and Tilly was thrilled that she and Sir Woof-alot got to have a sleepover with Cookie at her grandmother's.

'You look lovely,' James said when he collected Jenny.

'Thank you. You don't scrub up so badly yourself, Dr Madden,' she said with a smile.

He smiled back in acknowledgement, hoping that tonight he'd get the chance to be close to her and tell her how he really felt about her.

As he expected, she got on well with his old colleague and his family, and Tom took him to one side when Jenny went to the ladies'.

'I'm so glad you came tonight, James. And I like your Jenny.'

She wasn't really his Jenny—not yet, anyway.

But Tom didn't give him the chance to protest. 'She's lovely. She's perfect for you—and Anna would've liked her very much.'

'Yeah.' He had a lump in his throat. 'It's still early days.'

'The way you look at each other,' Tom said, 'it's obvious where this is going. And I'm really pleased for you. You deserve a bit of happiness.'

'Thanks,' James said, clapping him on the back. And he needed the subject changed before Jenny came back; he didn't want to risk her being spooked by the conversation. 'Now, I need to buy the ancient birthday boy a drink.'

Tom laughed, as James had hoped, and let himself be taken to the bar.

When Jenny came back, they spent the rest of the evening dancing to the kind of music that had always filled the floor in their student days. And then, at last, the DJ slowed everything down. Finally, Jenny was in his arms, just the way James had been aching for her to be all evening. He held her close, swaying with her to the music.

Was she, too, remembering the evening they'd danced by the waterfall?

Was she, too, remembering the night they'd

made love and then sat in the garden, watching the stars come out?

It was a risk—but he had nothing left to lose. If she said no, he'd still be in the friend zone, where he was languishing right now. If she said yes...

His heart rate sped up. Please let her say yes.

'It's a bit stuffy in here,' he said when the tempo of the music went up again. 'Want to come and get some fresh air?'

She nodded, and he led her out of the crowded hall. Thankfully there was a quiet garden, and he was able to find them a more private space.

'Jenny.' He took her hand and lifted it to his mouth, pressing a kiss into the palm and folding his fingers over it. 'I wanted to tell you, I...' He chickened out of using the word he wanted to use. 'I like you.'

Her eyes were huge in the moonlight. 'I like you, too,' she said.

It encouraged him enough to tell her the truth. 'But it's more than that,' he said. 'This brushing up of my dating skills—it turns out there's only one person I want to date. And not just date, either.' He took a deep breath.

'I love you, Jenny. I want to make a family with you.'

'James.' Her voice was husky. 'I… We haven't really known each other that long.'

Technically, they'd known each other for decades. But he knew what she meant. 'It's long enough for me to be sure,' he said.

'I…' She blew out a breath. 'James, this whole thing scares me.'

'I know,' he said. 'All I need to know is how you feel. The complications don't matter, because if we work together we can find a way round them.'

Could it really be that easy?

Four little words. That was all she had to say.

Someone opened the door to the pub's function room, and the chorus of 'Three Little Birds' blared out.

It was almost like a sign, telling her to stop worrying. Of course everything would be all right. James had a point: they'd work together and find a way round all the tricky stuff.

'I love you, too,' she admitted. 'I'm scared, but I love you.'

He wrapped his arms round her. 'No need to be scared. I'm here. I'm not going away.'

He kissed her lightly. 'I never thought I'd be happy again, after I lost Anna. But then I came back to Burndale, and I met you, and the world was suddenly full of sunshine again. I told myself that you were my friend—but you're so much more than that.'

'James.' Her heart was too full for words. Instead, she kissed him.

When he finally broke the kiss, he stroked her face. 'I need to get you home, Cinderella—and, much as I'd like to take you back to my house and have you all to myself for a while, I know Tamsin's waiting for us. We'll find time for us, later.'

He understood. He *really* understood. And she loved him even more for it.

When he dropped Jenny off in Burndale, Tamsin gave her a hug. 'You look happy,' she said.

Jenny nodded. 'James and I… I think it's going to work out.'

'Good.' Tamsin gave her another hug. 'For what it's worth, I think you're really well suited.'

'Me, too,' Jenny said. 'We're not going to rush things. But right now I feel happier than I have in years.'

The floating feeling was still there the next morning. Especially when James texted her.

Good morning. I love you.

She replied.

Good morning. I love you, too.

Happiness got her through the chores and even the bit of weeding she'd been avoiding in the back garden. She was smiling to herself, remembering the way James had kissed her, when she heard a yell.

The sound galvanised her into action; pulling off the gardening gloves as she went, she ran into the house.

Betty was on the floor in the kitchen.

'I tripped,' she said. 'I was making tea, and I tripped.'

'It's an accident. Nobody's fault,' Jenny reassured her. Though she knew it was her fault. She'd been mooning about over James instead of paying attention to her mum.

'I wanted to surprise you with a cup of tea.'

'That's lovely of you, Mum. Does anything hurt? Your arm? Your leg?' Jenny checked.

Reassured that there wasn't an obvious

fracture, she helped Betty to her feet and then to a chair.

'I'll make us that cup of tea, Mum,' she said.

Her mum was fine, apart from having a bit of a shock at the fall. But it could've been so much worse. Betty could've fallen and pulled the boiling kettle down and scalded herself. She could've hit her head on the corner of the table and given herself a subarachnoid haemorrhage. She could've ended up in hospital and then a nursing home, because she wasn't safe enough with Jenny.

And all because Jenny hadn't been paying proper attention.

Later that evening, when her mum was in bed, she video called James to tell him about Betty's fall. 'Thankfully, she's all right—but it's what *could* have happened that worries me.' She took a deep breath. 'James. I'm sorry. I can't offer you anything other than friendship.'

He frowned. 'Last night, you said you loved me.'

'I do,' she said. 'But Mum needs me more. I don't have room in my life for anything else. We can't see each other, any more.'

His face tightened. 'I think you're using your mother as an excuse.'

She glared at him. 'That's not fair.'

'I think, deep down, you're scared of having another relationship in case you make a mistake and you end up being hurt, the way Simon hurt you,' he said. 'And instead of seeing this as an accident that could've happened at any time, you're seizing on it as a reason to avoid seeing me.'

His words stung, and she lashed out. 'Says the man who hasn't tried to have a real relationship, since his wife died.'

'That,' he said, 'isn't quite true. I recognised I needed someone in my life and I wasn't in the right place to offer anyone a relationship. I asked you to help me work on my dating skills.'

'I'm glad you're admitting that nothing between us was real,' she said tightly.

'Oh, but it was,' he said. 'It started out as friendship and it quickly became something more. I fell in love with you, Jenny, and you admitted that you feel the same way about me.'

'Mum has to come first,' she repeated stubbornly.

'I'm not saying she doesn't,' he said, raking

his hand through his hair. 'In any true partnership, there's give and take. There's compromise. Sometimes you have to put someone else's needs first for a while. There will be times when we need to put your mum first, and times when we need to put Tilly first. And there will be times when we put *us* first,' he said.

She shook her head. 'I don't have the headspace for this. I can't be with you any more.'

'You're being a coward,' James said.

'That's unfair.'

'Is it? I think you're scared because deep down you believe I'll let you down, the way Simon did. But you're not giving me the chance to show you that I'm not like Simon.'

'And I'm not Anna,' she said, nettled.

'I don't expect you to be like Anna. You're *you*. And I've learned to face my fear of losing someone again—it probably won't be to an amniotic embolism, but it could be to a road accident, a virus, or something completely out of the blue. I've come to realise that if I try to avoid the risk of losing someone by keeping myself locked away, I'm actually losing far more. Anna would've quoted the Tennyson thing about it being better to have loved and lost than never to have loved at all. And it's true. It hurts when you lose someone,' he said, 'but it hurts you a lot more if you lock yourself away and don't give yourself the chance to open your life up to love.'

She knew he had a point, but she couldn't get past her worries. 'I can't do this, James.'

He sighed. 'All right. Talk to me again when you're ready to face your fears,' he said.

But she couldn't, she thought as she ended the call.

She was stuck.

CHAPTER TEN

'ARE WE SEEING Jenny and Betty, tonight, Daddy?' Tilly asked, several days later.

'No.'

'Why not?'

'They're busy, sweetheart,' James said.

'What about tomorrow?'

He shook his head, hating the way the light dimmed in his daughter's face as it sank in that they wouldn't be seeing Jenny any time soon.

'But I taught Woofy to sit and stay,' she said, sounding devastated. 'I want to show them how clever he is.'

'I know, darling,' James said.

He needed to fix things between himself and Jenny so they could at least go back to some kind of friendship.

But she was barely talking to him, except at work. And even then, it was only when they were both working on a patient. Like the dog they'd worked on this morning, who'd eaten a knuckle bone at the weekend and then started vomiting, and the worried owners had found bone shards in the dog's vomit and diarrhoea.

Jenny had felt a firm mass in the dog's intestines, and thought maybe some of the knuckle bone had become lodged in the dog's bowels. She'd asked James to handle the sedation for an X-ray, which revealed a blockage in the dog's intestines; he'd deepened the sedation to full anaesthesia so Jenny could remove the blockage before it ruptured the dog's bowel. Given a few days, the dog would make a full recovery.

His relationship with Jenny had a far less certain prognosis.

Jenny took a second reading with the no-contact forehead thermometer. Despite Jenny getting her mum to take sips of water, sponging her face and arms with tepid water to cool her skin down and patting it dry, and giving her mum paracetamol, Betty's temperature was still climbing. It was above thirty-eight degrees centigrade now, so it definitely counted as fever.

And Betty was getting agitated, mumbling to herself.

The GP's surgery and the local pharmacy were both closed, so Jenny couldn't ring them for advice. The chances were, this was another urinary tract infection—Betty had had them before. Jenny knew they were more common among elderly women, because their urine flow was weaker and the bladder didn't empty completely, which could lead to a build-up of bacteria. A UTI could cause confusion—and infections could also speed up the progress of dementia. Betty had bounced back from the last one, but she hadn't been as agitated.

Her brother was two hours away, but he would at least listen and give her some professional advice, enough to stop her panicking.

'Rob? I think Mum might have a UTI. She's got a temperature, and she's a bit agitated and confused,' she said.

'When did you last give her paracetamol?'

'Two hours ago, and her temperature's still climbing. I'm getting her to take sips of water, but I've got a bad feeling about this.'

'I think you're right and it's probably a UTI,' Robert said. 'I'd try and get a urine sample, if you can, then get her to the emergency department. If it's a UTI, they'll give her antibiotics. Don't wait until your GP's surgery opens tomorrow.'

'OK,' she said.

'Do you want me to come over?'

'It's fine,' she said. 'I know you're busy.'

'Keep me posted,' he said, 'and if you need me to talk to anyone, call me. I'll make sure my phone's free.'

'Thanks, Rob.'

She called an ambulance, only to be told that there would be a three-hour wait.

The quicker she could get her mum diagnosed, and treated with antibiotics if her suspicion that it was a UTI was correct, the better.

'Come on, Mum. I'm going to take you to see a doctor to make you feel better.'

'We can't go until the coalman's been paid,' Betty said, twisting her hands together.

Coal? It must be several decades since her mother had lived in a house heated by coal. Clearly she was stuck in the past, not knowing where she was now.

'It's all right. I'll pay the bill over the phone,' Jenny said, wanting to reassure her mum.

She put Betty's shoes on, texted their neighbour Sheila to say that she was taking Betty to hospital and would keep her posted, texted Robert to say she was taking their mum to hospital, and drove to the hospital in Harrogate.

The staff at the emergency department triaged Betty, took the urine sample and tested it, and admitted her to a ward for treatment with antibiotics and a drip to get fluids into her. Jenny stepped outside for long enough to call Rob and Sheila with an update, and to let Archer know she wouldn't be in for her usual Wednesday morning session, then went back to her mother's side.

'Go home and get some rest, love,' the senior sister advised.

Jenny shook her head. 'Mum's confused, and I don't want to add to the worry. At least if she sees me, she'll know she's here for a reason.' She gave the nurse a wry smile. 'And if I go home I'll drive myself crackers, worrying about her. I'd rather be here.'

On Wednesday, James came in to Burndale Veterinary Surgery, prepared for another difficult day working with Jenny, only to discover that she was at her mum's bedside in hospital.

'Do you know how Betty is?' he asked Archer.

'They're struggling to get her temperature down, Jenny said this morning,' Archer said.

'She must be worried sick.' And, being Jenny, she'd be dealing with it on her own.

He quickly texted her.

Archer told me about Betty being in hospital. Give her our love. Anything I can do to help, let me know. Will pick up messages after surgery. J x

Her reply was polite.

Thank you.

It told him nothing.

But there was one person who might know more. He rang Sheila, who told him Jenny was staying at the hospital until Betty improved. 'If you talk to her, tell her I'm feeding Sooty for them and keeping an eye on the house.'

'I will,' he promised, and called his mum.

'Of course you need to go and see them,' Christine said. 'I'll collect Tilly from nursery.'

'Thanks, Mum. I owe you,' James said.

After he'd seen his last patient and sorted out the paperwork, he headed for the supermarket to pick up some grapes and some lemon barley water for Betty—most hospitals had a policy of not allowing flowers— and a card, then drove to Harrogate.

He called in to the geriatric ward and checked with the nurse on Reception, who directed him to Betty's ward.

Jenny was sitting by her mother's bed, holding Betty's hand; there were deep shadows beneath her eyes. She clearly hadn't slept, the previous night.

'Hey,' he said. 'I know sometimes when you're not well, it tempts you to drink if there's something flavouring the water, so I bought Betty some lemon barley and some grapes.'

'Thank you.' She bit her lip. 'I didn't expect to see you.'

'And you didn't ask me to come. I know. But I thought you could do with a bit of support. Which is exactly what you'd do for me, if I was in your shoes,' he said, before she could start arguing. 'When did you last eat?'

She shook her head. 'I'm not hungry.'

'So not since yesterday. OK. See you in a bit.'

He headed for the cafeteria and bought her a cup of strong tea, a chicken salad sandwich and a banana. He added a chocolate brownie, and went back to the ward.

Her eyes widened as she saw him. He smiled, put the food on Betty's bedside cabinet, then fetched another chair. 'Move,' he said. 'I'll hold Betty's hand while you eat that sandwich and drink your tea.'

'But—'

'Not buts,' he said firmly. 'You need to

look after yourself as well, Jenny. If you're not well, how are you going to be able to look after your mum properly?'

She clearly couldn't argue with his logic, so she gave in, muttering her thanks.

James chatted to Betty, telling her all about Sir Woofalot and how Tilly was doing at nursery, until Jenny had finished her sandwich and the tea.

To his relief, the colour in her face was slightly better.

'Now, your mum needs to rest,' he said, 'and she's not going to be able to do that if she's worrying about you. So this is the deal, Jenny. I'm driving you back to Burndale now, and I'll drive you back here in the morning before I go to work. It's up to you whether you want to go back to your own house, stay at mine, or stay at my mum's, but you are most definitely going to sleep in a bed tonight instead of half dozing on an uncomfortable chair for the second night in a row.'

'But Mum—'

'Is in the best hands,' he said firmly.

'What about Tilly?'

'It's fine. Mum or Vicky will drop her at nursery tomorrow. That's what families do, pitch in and help when it's needed,' he added softly. 'You need to get some rest. Otherwise you're going to be too exhausted to sit with your mum tomorrow. You need a shower and a comfortable bed.'

Colour slashed across her cheeks, and he realised how she might have taken his words.

'That's not me trying to get you to sleep with me,' he said swiftly. 'I mean you need to rest. Your mum's asleep now, and there's nothing you can do apart from wait for the antibiotics to kick in. Say goodnight to her, and I'm driving you back to Burndale.'

Clearly wanting to stay, but also knowing that he had a point, Jenny kissed her mum's forehead. 'Night, Mum. I'll be back in the morning.'

'And I'll keep an eye on your girl, Betty,' James added.

'My car's still here. I'll drive myself,' Jenny said.

'You're shattered. Don't drive tonight,' he said. 'I'll take you wherever you want to go, and I'll pick you up tomorrow and bring you back here.'

He was as good as his word, taking Jenny back to her own house, then feeding Sooty and making her a mug of hot chocolate with hot milk while she had a shower, changed into her pyjamas and wrapped herself in a fluffy towelling dressing gown.

'Lock up behind me, drink the chocolate and go to bed,' he said firmly.

'What if the hospital calls and says Mum's worse?' Without her car, she'd have to rely on a taxi, and she didn't want to waste time that her mum might not have.

'Then you ring me, and I'll drive you in,' he said, cutting through the jumble of fears in her head. 'Goodnight, Jenny.'

And then, the bit that made her tears spill over after he'd left, he gave her a hug and kissed the top of her head. 'Betty's in the right place. I bet in the morning you'll see a difference in her. Get some rest, and things will look better tomorrow.'

Jenny thought she'd never be able to sleep, for worrying about her mum; but she made herself close her eyes and, perhaps worn out from her vigil by Betty's bedside, she fell asleep almost instantly.

The next morning, she was up and ready before James arrived, called the hospital to see how her mum was doing, and had just boiled the kettle when James rapped on the kitchen door and walked in.

'Breakfast,' he said, handing her a bacon roll. 'Because I'm guessing you haven't eaten anything this morning.'

'Not yet,' she admitted.

'How's your mum doing?'

'She had a good night, but her temperature's still up and she's still not making sense.'

'You and I both know that's a common side-effect of a UTI and it can take time for antibiotics to kick in,' he said. 'It doesn't mean her dementia's suddenly taken a dive.'

But it was still a possibility, one she dreaded. When that day came, she'd need to give up her job completely for a while. Instead, she said, 'The kettle's boiled. Can I make you a mug of coffee?'

'If you've got a travel mug, that would be lovely,' he said. 'Thank you.'

He came up to the ward with her to see Betty, then kissed her mother on the cheek and told Jenny he'd be back after work.

'You really don't have to come,' she said. 'I had a good night's sleep. I'm safe to drive myself home.'

'OK,' he said. 'Provided you promise you'll call me if you need anything.'

'I will. And thank you for everything you've done.'

Her brother Robert arrived at lunchtime. 'I got a locum for this afternoon,' he said.

She bit back the comment that it was about time he'd made the effort. 'I'll give you some time alone with Mum,' she said, and headed for the cafeteria.

He came to find her, an hour later. 'Mum's asleep—before you ask, that's the only reason I left. And I don't want to have this conversation with you in the ward, in case she wakes up and overhears.'

'What conversation?' she asked, her stomach dipping.

'Jen, when she's recovered from this, I think she's going to need more help than you can give her.'

Jenny shook her head. 'She'll be fine when she's over the infection and comes home.'

'Jen, you need to face this. She has dementia, and she's not going to get better,' he said. 'Every day, we're going to lose a bit more of her. Some days she'll be on an even keel, and other days she'll dip down further.'

'I know.' Did he think she was stupid? As soon as their mum had been diagnosed, she'd read up on the condition.

'She needs nursing care.'

'Where she'll be stuck in a chair in front of

a television, in a room that's way too hot so it keeps her quiet? No.'

He sighed. 'Not all nursing homes are like that.'

'They don't want to be like that, I know—but they have to manage with not enough staff. I promised Mum I'd never put her in a nursing home,' Jenny said. 'I intend to keep that promise, Rob. Even if she gets to the stage where she doesn't know where she is, *I'll* know—and that's what counts. I can look after Mum myself. She's at day-care three days a week, while I'm at work, and the rest of the time I can look after her. It's fine.'

'It's not fine,' Robert said. 'It's a really heavy burden, being a full-time carer and working. You've got yourself to think of, too.'

She noticed that he didn't offer to share the care. Then again, he lived two hours away and had teenage children to think of.

'I'm fine as I am,' she said. 'If you've come here to have a fight, I'm not interested. I think you should go home, now.'

'Jen—' he protested.

'No, really. Just go home, Rob.' She stood up, put her hands on her hips and glared at him. 'I'm the one who's been looking after Mum for the last couple of years. You ring her once a week, visit once a month if she's lucky—so, no, you don't get to swan in and tell me what to do. Go home.'

He glared back at her, then muttered something rude and stomped out of the café.

And Jenny was so fed up with being bossed about that when James texted her to ask if there was anything she needed, she snapped back her reply.

Nothing, thank you. I appreciate your kindness earlier but we don't need any help.

Something had clearly upset Jenny, James thought, looking at the text—hopefully nothing he'd done or said. But when she pushed him away for the third day in a row, he was at a loss what to do.

'It's impossible. She's putting a brick wall round herself,' he said to Archer, handing his friend a mug of tea after surgery had finished.

'She's worried about her mum,' Archer said. 'Give her time.'

'Time to make that brick wall even higher, and maybe add climb proof paint and a bit of barbed wire?' James asked.

'There is that,' Archer said. 'What's actually going on with you and Jenny?'

'We have...feelings for each other,' James said. 'More than friendship.'

Archer grinned. 'Yeah. I know that one.'

'You and Halley.' James smiled ruefully. 'I envy you.'

'She taught me I need to reach for the dream,' Archer said. 'Maybe you can learn from me. If Jenny's your dream, then what are the obstacles?'

'I think the real obstacle's Jenny herself,' James said. 'She seems to have this idea that she has to do everything herself, on her own—whereas in a proper relationship you support each other.'

'You know the situation with her ex,' Archer said. 'He left her to do everything—and he wanted her to move to London with him when he knew she was worried about her mum.'

James frowned. 'But I'm not her ex. She knows that.'

'Talk to her,' Archer advised. 'Be honest. It's all you can do.'

The hospital really wasn't the right place to have a conversation with her but, short of stalking her house, how would he know when she was actually home?

Maybe it was time to enlist some help.

He asked his sister to pick up Tilly, bought some flowers, and went to see Jenny's neighbour.

Later that evening, Sheila rang him. 'She's just got home from the hospital, love. See if you can talk some sense into her,' she said.

'Thank you. I'll try,' James said.

He drove over and knocked on Jenny's kitchen door.

She looked bone-deep tired and miserable when she answered.

'Not now,' she said.

'Jenny, have you eaten today?' he asked.

She sighed. 'Don't nag, James. I'm not in the mood to cook.'

He lifted up the tote bag he'd brought with him. 'I guessed as much. Which is why I brought you a tub of home-made pasta with pesto, chicken and grilled peppers,' he said. 'Works hot or cold. Let me in, and I'll stick it in a bowl for you and get you a drink.'

'You're not going to take no for an answer, are you?' she asked wryly.

'Absolutely not,' he said. 'No more talking

until you've eaten. Do you want the pasta hot or cold?'

She closed her eyes momentarily, as if she was giving in. 'Cold, please.'

He scooped the salad into a bowl, fished cutlery out of the drawer and made her sit at the kitchen table. Jenny took a couple of mouthfuls, clearly intending to be polite, but then polished off the lot.

'Thank you. That was really…' A tear leaked down her face, and she scrubbed it away crossly. 'Ignore that. I'm fine.'

'Jenny, you've had days of worry about your mum. Nobody would be fine, in your shoes. And you don't have to be fine. I'm here.'

'You don't have time. You're a single dad.'

'With a supportive family who lives nearby.' Exactly what she didn't have.

A muscle worked in her jaw. 'Rob thinks I should put Mum in a home. He says I can't look after her on my own.'

'He has a point,' James said.

Her eyes sparked in outrage. 'I think you'd better leave. Now.'

'Hear me out,' he said. 'You're running yourself ragged right now, working and look- ing after your mum. I know you love her, and

I know you want the best for her. But what happens to your mum if you get the flu, say?'

'I'll sort something out.' She folded her arms and glared at him.

'I'm not saying you should put Betty in full-time care. What I'm saying is that you can't do it all on your own. You need support. I learned something, the other day.'

She frowned. 'Where are you going with this?'

James reminded himself that this wasn't the real Jenny. Right now she was tired, worried sick and over-burdened, and that was why she was snapping at him. 'I finally got round to finishing the unpacking, the other day. When I was putting the books on the shelves, a post-card Anna had been using as a bookmark fell out. It had a quote from John Donne—her favourite poet—on it. "No man is an island." I think you're trying to be an island, Jenny, doing everything yourself.'

She rolled her eyes. 'That's how it is.'

'But it doesn't have to be.' He sighed. 'I'm making a mess of this. What I'm trying to say—without putting any extra pressure on you—is that I want to be a family with you. Being apart from you, these last few days, has really brought it home to me how important you are to me. I've missed you—at work, and outside.'

Her eyes filled with tears. 'I've missed you, too.'

'Then stop pushing me away. I love you, and you've admitted you love me. Let's make a life together.'

'It's too complicated,' she said quietly.

'Is it? Because I think we could make this work. You, me, Betty and Tilly. We'll support each other. Tilly gets a mum who can do all the girly stuff with her that I can't. Betty gets a son-in-law who'll spend time with her and can lift her when she needs it. And you and I—we get each other,' he said with a smile. 'We get to fall asleep in each other's arms, and wake up in each other's arms. We get our private moments. We might need to sneak them in, sometimes, but that's all part of being a family.'

She looked at him as if she couldn't quite believe it was possible.

'You and I, we're not islands,' he said. 'We both come as a package. And, yes, we'll need to move—but to a place that has a ground-floor bedroom and a wet room for Betty, and where she'll be part of a bigger family. Where we all contribute. And where we're together because we love each other.'

She swallowed hard. 'You'd do that for me?'

'*We'd* do this for *us*. All of us,' he corrected. 'As for Sooty and Sir Woofalot—they might be a bit wary of each other at first, but they'll learn to rub along. Just like we will. It's what being a family means.' He smiled. 'We can have it all, Jenny. All I need from you is one little word. I love you. Will you marry me?'

He meant it.

And, as she stared at him, the penny finally dropped. He wasn't like Simon. He meant it about being there for her. About being a partnership. A team. A family.

And that knowledge was enough to dissolve her fears.

'I love you, James,' she said. 'Yes.'

'About time, too,' he said, and kissed her.

EPILOGUE

One year later

'NANA BETTY! I made a picture of you and me and Sooty and Woofy,' Tilly said, scampering into the open-plan kitchen/living room in front of her father and handing a picture to Betty, who was sitting in a chair by the French windows overlooking the garden. She'd labelled the figures painstakingly in wobbly handwriting.

'That's lovely, Jenny,' Betty said.

'I'm Tilly,' Tilly corrected with a smile. 'Jenny's my mum.'

'Certainly am, lambkin,' Jenny said, bending down to give the little girl a hug and a kiss hello.

Tilly had asked her if she could call her 'Mum' the day that she and James had told the little girl that they wanted to get married and make a family together, and over the last year Jenny had discovered how much joy a little girl could bring into her life—and her mother's. 'That's a beautiful picture. Where do you want to put it?'

'Nana Betty's room?' Tilly said.

'No. Keep it here,' Betty said. 'Where everyone can see it. Put it on the…thingy.' She waved a hand towards the kitchen area, to indicate she couldn't quite remember the word.

'Fridge,' James supplied, kissing her cheek. 'Good idea, Betty. Go and see where we've got a space, Tilly, and I'll lift you up so you can stick your drawing to the fridge with a magnet.' He turned to his wife to kiss her. 'Good day?' he asked quietly.

'More than good,' she said, her voice equally quiet. 'I have news for you.'

'What kind of news?'

'Complicated,' she said. 'Or it will be, in about seven months.'

James's eyes widened as he worked out what she meant. 'That's the best kind of news,' he said. 'I know Tilly still wants a white kitten called Twinkle, but I think she'll settle for having a little brother or sister. Betty will love having a baby around.' He kissed her. 'And I didn't think you could possibly make me any happier, but you have. I'm the luckiest man in the world.'

'We're the luckiest family in the world,' she corrected. 'Because we have each other.'

'We have each other,' he agreed.

* * * * *

If you missed the previous story in the Yorkshire Village Vets duet, then check out

Bound by Their Pregnancy Surprise
by Louisa Heaton

And if you enjoyed this story, check out these other great reads from Kate Hardy

An English Vet in Paris
Saving Christmas for the ER Doc
Surgeon's Second Chance in Florence

All available now!